A figure emerged from the shadows. A man.

He wore jeans and boots and a black cowboy hat pulled low over his brow.

Even so, she instantly recognized him, and her broken heart beat like it was brand-new.

Sam! He was back. After nine years.

Why? And what was he doing at the Gold Nugget?

"Annie?" He started down the stairs, the confused expression on his face changing to one of recognition. "It's you!"

Suddenly nervous, she retreated. If he hadn't seen her, she'd have run.

No, that was a stupid reaction. She wasn't young and vulnerable anymore. She was thirty-four. The mother of a three-year-old child. Grown. Confident. Strong.

And yet, the door beckoned. He'd always had that effect on her, been able to strip away her defenses.

A rush of irritation, more at herself than him, galvanized her. "What are you doing here?"

Dear Reader,

I always love starting a new series. It's kind of like decorating a barren room or planning a huge event. There are so many possibilities, and exploring them is fun and exciting. I get to decide where the series takes place, what about this particular community makes it unusual and interesting, and, most important, who are the characters that will inhabit it? I'm not sure what part appeals to me the most.

I visited Lake Tahoe and the surrounding area many years ago and was struck by its rugged beauty. I left thinking that someday I would set a book there. The chance didn't come until now. Sweetheart, Nevada, is based loosely on the area north of Lake Tahoe. And here's a secret just between you and me. The Gold Nugget Ranch featured in my book is inspired by the Ponderosa Ranch where the TV series *Bonanza* was filmed. Promise not to tell?

With a name like Sweetheart, you can count on a lot of romance. But the road won't be easy for Sam and Annie, my struggling couple in *The Rancher's Homecoming*. In addition to rebuilding a relationship that went wrong years ago, they are fighting to save their town after a devastating wildfire nearly destroyed it. The situation is further complicated by their young daughters, Annie's charming yet difficult mother and grandmother, and a menagerie of orphaned animals.

As always, I love hearing from readers. You can contact me at cathy@cathymcdavid.com.

Warmest wishes,

Cathy McDavid

The Rancher's Homecoming

CATHY McDAVID

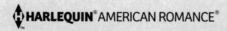

Recycling programs
for this product may
not exist in your area.

ISBN-13: 978-0-373-75462-5

THE RANCHER'S HOMECOMING

Copyright © 2013 by Cathy McDavid

Printed in U.S.A.

ABOUT THE AUTHOR

Cathy makes her home in Scottsdale, Arizona, near the breathtaking McDowell Mountains, where hawks fly overhead, javelina traipse across her front yard and mountain lions occasionally come calling. She embraced the country life at an early age, acquiring her first horse in eighth grade. Dozens of horses followed through the years, along with mules, an obscenely fat donkey, chickens, ducks, goats and a potbellied pig who had her own swimming pool. Nowadays, two spoiled dogs and two spoiled-er cats round out the McDavid pets. Cathy loves contemporary and historical ranch stories and often incorporates her own experiences into her books.

When not writing, Cathy and her family and friends spend as much time as they can at her cabin in the small town of Young. Of course, she takes her laptop with her on the chance inspiration strikes.

Books by Cathy McDavid
HARLEQUIN AMERICAN ROMANCE

Chapter One

Six weeks since the fire and the lingering smell of smoke still burned like acid in the back of her throat. Annie Hennessy covered her mouth and nose, remembering the days immediately following the fire when they were forced to wear face masks and hazmat suits as they waded through the waist-deep ruins of the inn that had been in her family for the past fifty years.

Like then, she bit back the sobs, afraid even letting one escape would cause her to break down entirely. Where would she and her daughter be then? Her mother and grandmother? Homeless, probably. Or living on the generosity of some relative.

Annie took a tentative step forward, wincing as something crunched beneath the sole of her hiking boot. She dreaded looking down but did anyway.

The charred remains of a picture frame lay in her path, barely recognizable. Whichever room the painting had once hung in was anyone's guess. During the fire, the roof caved in on the second floor, which had then collapsed onto the first floor.

Only the foundation, parts of the exterior walls and a few blackened ceiling beams remained. All the precious heirlooms, antiques, furnishings and mementoes the Hennessy women had collected over the past half century had been reduced to a giant pile of rubble in a matter of minutes.

No, not everything. As Annie took another step forward, something metallic peeked out from beneath a plank of wood.

Squatting down, she shoved aside the plank, mindless of the grime smearing her hands. One by one, her fingers closed around the object, and her pulse quickened. Why hadn't she noticed this before today?

Like a miner discovering a diamond in a barren field, she unearthed the discolored desk bell and held it up to catch the late-afternoon sunlight streaming in from overhead. For as long as she could remember, this bell had sat atop the lobby desk. Hundreds, no, thousands of guests had rung it.

Another piece of Annie's shattered heart broke off.

She clutched the bell to her chest and waited for the strength to rise in her. She would add this to her collection of salvaged treasures. A metal comb, a silver teapot, an iron hinge to the storeroom door, to name a few.

Annie fought her way across the piles of crumbling debris covering the former lobby floor. Staying here another minute was impossible. Why did she insist on torturing herself by stopping every day on her drive home from work?

Because *this* was her home. Not the tiny two-bedroom apartment in town where she and her family currently resided.

Bracing her free hand on the front entrance door frame, she propelled herself through the opening and across the lawn, filling her lungs with much-needed clean air.

Her SUV stood where she'd left it, in what had been the inn's parking lot. The vehicle, a pea-green all-wheel-drive monstrosity, bore the logo of the Nevada Division of Forestry on its driver's side door.

Annie had started working for the NDF only last week and considered herself one of the lucky few. She'd gotten a job, low paying as it was. Too many of her friends and fellow residents were unable to find employment or even a place to live.

For the Hennessys' inn wasn't the only structure in Sweetheart, Nevada, that succumbed to the fire's insatiable hunger. Nine thousand acres of pristine mountain wilderness and two-thirds of the town's homes and businesses were destroyed—along with *all* of their livelihoods and very way of life.

Once behind the wheel, Annie didn't head to the apartment. Instead, she took the road out of town. Her mother wasn't expecting her for another hour. And as much as Annie wanted to see her beautiful daughter, she needed a few moments of solitude in a place that had escaped the fire. A place where her spirit could mend.

She slapped the visor down as she turned west. Before the fire, she hadn't needed to shade her eyes. The towering ponderosa pines on both sides of the road would have blocked the sun's glare. Now, a sea of scorched trunks and branches stretched for miles. Every hundred feet or so, a single tree stood, lush and green and miraculously spared.

What Annie wouldn't give to have her family's inn be like those surviving trees.

This wasn't just the town where she'd grown up and the inn her place of work. Her roots ran deep. According to her grandmother, the Hennessy line went all the way back to the first settlers.

Shortly after the gold rush of 1849, a wagon train passed through the Sierra Nevada Mountains. On it, two young passengers met and fell in love. When the wagon train stopped in what was now Sweetheart, the man proposed to the woman. They married in California but returned to the spot where they'd become engaged to settle and raise a family. The next year, the man discovered gold. Word traveled and people arrived. The small town that sprang up was called Sweetheart after its first settlers and founders of the mine.

Many of the businesses in town, including Annie's family's, capitalized on the legend. To Annie, it was more than just a story, it was her heritage.

Ten minutes later, she stopped the SUV at the security gate blocking the entrance to the Gold Nugget Ranch and got out. Several years earlier, after the ranch had been closed to the public, the caretaker had entrusted Annie's family with a spare key. She was supposed to use it only for emergencies.

She considered mending her broken spirit as good an emergency as any.

To her surprise, she found the gate closed but padlock hanging open. Had Emmett been here and forgotten to secure the lock when he left? Doubtful. The caretaker was as dependable as ants at a picnic. But what other explanation could there be?

Returning to her SUV, she navigated the steep and winding mile-long dirt road to the ranch. Even before she got there, she spotted an unfamiliar Chevy dually pickup parked near the sprawling front porch.

The truck was empty. So was the porch. Whoever was here must be inside or out back. But why would they have a key to the gate?

Annie strode determinedly across the dirt and gravel yard to the porch steps. Every inch of the house and grounds was familiar to her. Not only had she visited on countless occasions, she'd seen it over and over while watching syndicated reruns of *The Forty-Niners* on TV.

The front door stood partially ajar and creaked loudly when she pushed it open. Her footsteps echoed ghostlike as she crossed the empty parlor.

"Hello? Anybody here?"

She should be nervous. The stranger prowling the house or grounds might be a vandal or a thief or even an ax murderer. Except what ax murderer drove a fire-engine-red pickup truck?

Maybe a real estate agent was here showing the ranch to a prospective buyer. It had been for sale the past several years, though there had been few lookers and no serious offers. Despite the ranch's claim to fame—a location used to film *The Forty-Niners* for eight years during the late '60s and early '70s—and a much reduced price, it was a bit of a white elephant.

Annie was secretly glad. For as long as she could remember, it had been her dream to buy the iconic ranch.

Since the fire, her only dream was to survive each day.

At a noise from above, she started toward the staircase. "Hello!" Taking hold of the dusty newel post, she let her gaze travel the steps to the second floor.

A figure emerged from the shadows. A man. He wore jeans and boots and a black cowboy hat was pulled low over his brow.

Even so, she instantly recognized him, and her damaged heart beat as though it was brand-new.

Sam! He was back. After nine years.

Why? And what was he doing at the Gold Nugget?

"Annie?" He started down the stairs, the confused expression on his face changing to one of recognition. "It's you!"

Suddenly nervous, she retreated. If he hadn't seen her, she'd have run.

No, that was a stupid reaction. She wasn't young and vulnerable anymore. She was thirty-four. The mother of a three-year-old child. Grown. Confident. Strong.

And yet, the door beckoned. He'd always had that effect on her, been able to strip away her defenses.

A rush of irritation, more at herself than him, galvanized her. "What are you doing here?"

Ignoring her question, he descended the stairs, his boots making contact with the wooden steps one at a time. Lord, it seemed to take forever.

This wasn't, she recalled, the first time he'd kept her waiting. Or the longest.

At last he stood before her, tall, handsome and every inch the rugged cowboy she remembered.

"Hey, girl, how are you? I wasn't sure you still lived in Sweetheart."

He spoke with an ease that gave no hint of those last angry words they'd exchanged. He even used his once familiar endearment for her and might have swept her into a hug if Annie didn't step to the side.

"Still here."

"I heard about the inn." Regret filled his voice. "I'm sorry."

"Me, too." She lifted her chin. "We're going to rebuild. As soon as we settle with the insurance company."

"You look good." His gaze never left her face, for which she was glad. He didn't seem to notice her rumpled and soiled khaki uniform. Her hair escaping her ponytail and hanging in limp tendrils. Her lack of makeup. "Th-thank you."

"Been a while."

"Quite a while."

His blue eyes transfixed her, as they always had, and she felt her bones melt.

Dammit! Her entire world had fallen apart the past six weeks. She didn't need Sam showing up, kicking at the pieces.

"What are you doing here?" she said, repeating her earlier question. "How did you get in?"

"The real estate agent gave me the keys." He held them up in an offering of proof, his potent grin disarming her. "I always liked this place."

He had. They'd come here often when they were dating. She'd show him the areas off-limits to tourists, all the while going on and on about her plans to buy the ranch and turn it into a bed-and-breakfast. Plans Sam had shared.

Now he was here, holding the keys.

He couldn't possibly be interested in purchasing the place. He lived in Northern California. Worked there. Had a wife and daughter there, the last she'd heard.

"How's your mom and grandmother?" he asked.

"Fine." She wouldn't admit the truth. None of them were

fine after losing everything and they wore their scars each in their own way. "I have a daughter now. She's three."

His smile changed and became softer. "I'm happy for you. You always wanted kids. Your husband from Sweetheart?"

"Yes." She swallowed. "We're not married anymore." Good grief. What had possessed her to admit that?

"A shame." Emotions difficult to read flashed in his eyes. "Losing a spouse is hard."

He said it as if he had firsthand experience.

"I'm managing," she admitted. "*We're* managing."

"Maybe you can let me in on the secret."

"You're divorced?"

"Widowed. My wife died a year and a half ago."

"Oh, Sam." Her heart nearly stopped.

"A drunk driver ran the light."

She'd never known the woman but felt bad for the late Mrs. Wyler and for Sam. Having one's life implode was something she understood.

"That must have been awful for you."

He nodded and glanced toward the empty kitchen with its large picture window. "My daughter's here with me. She's out back. I should probably find her. I told the real estate agent I'd meet her in town at five to sign the papers."

Sign the papers! Even as Annie's mind formed the thought, he spoke it out loud.

"We're scheduled to close escrow tomorrow. I'm the new owner of the Gold Nugget."

SAM FOLLOWED ANNIE out onto the porch, only to pause and watch her as she composed herself. He hadn't thought she'd take the news of him buying the Gold Nugget so hard. The sight of her features crumbling would stay with him always.

He leaned his back against one of the thick columns, giving her space. Like the ranch house and barn, the columns were constructed from indigenous pines harvested when the land was originally cleared. According to the plaque mounted by the entrance, that occurred more than two decades before ground was broken on the Sweetheart Inn.

He should, he realized much too late, have chosen his words more kindly. Annie loved the Gold Nugget almost as much as she did her family's inn. He'd been surprised to see the ranch listed for sale, assuming she and her mother would have purchased it years ago.

Annie had always been able to trip him up without even trying. A glance, a touch, a softly whispered response and his concentration went out the window.

Nine years, and she still had that effect on him.

Maybe buying the Gold Nugget wasn't such a good idea after all.

Sam instantly changed his mind. He'd returned to Sweetheart with a purpose, and unintentionally hurting Annie's feelings wouldn't stop him from fulfilling it.

"I'd like to see you while I'm here."

She halted midstep and sent him a look intended to cut him down to size.

"Not a date," he clarified. "To catch up. And to pick your brain."

"I have enough on my plate with rebuilding the inn," she answered tersely. "You can't expect me to be a part of whatever it is you've planned for the ranch."

"Not just the ranch. The entire town, too, and the people in it."

"I don't understand."

"I want to help, Annie."

Unaffected by his attempted sincerity, she narrowed her green eyes. "With what?"

"Rebuilding Sweetheart."

"Is this a joke?"

"I've hired a construction contractor to remodel the Gold Nugget."

"Remodel it!"

"Into a working cattle ranch. One where the guests can enjoy the full cowboy experience, not just go on rides."

"Full cowboy experience?"

"Yeah. Herd cattle, vaccinate calves, repair fences, clear trails, clean stalls if they want. I'm also planning monthly roping and team penning competitions for the adults and gymkhanas for the kids."

She shook her head in disbelief. "What person would want to clean horse stalls on their vacation?"

"You'd be surprised."

He understood her reservations. All of the local businesses had depended on the wedding trade. Florist shop, tuxedo rental, wedding boutique, caterers, photographers. Not to mention restaurants specializing in romantic candlelit dinners or those with large banquet rooms for receptions.

A guest ranch would have been a ridiculous idea and unnecessary if not for the fire. The same fire that Sam and his crew of Hotshot firefighters had fought and failed to prevent from ravaging the town.

Not his crew. He alone was responsible.

His stomach still clenched at the memory of that day. His anger at his commanding officer, his fear for the citizens' safety, the helplessness he'd felt when the wind changed direction and the fire leaped the ravine. The sorrow for all that was lost and could have been saved.

"There are only a handful of really great working guest ranches in this part of the country. Add to that the popularity of *The Forty-Niners,* and I think the ranch will be booked to capacity year-round."

"No, it won't. Sweetheart is where people come to get married. We perform a hundred wedding ceremonies every month."

"Where people *did* come. How many ceremonies have been performed since the fire?"

She clamped her mouth shut, saying nothing. No need for it; they both knew the answer. Zero. A measly six weeks had passed and already Sweetheart was dying on the vine. Without a miracle, it would wither away into nothing.

Sam wasn't about to let that happen and possessed the drive and the resources to prevent it.

"I can change that. Bring the tourists back. I'll also be able to provide jobs for some of the locals. From what the real estate agent tells me, there's plenty who need work." His gaze involuntarily strayed to her work shirt and the NDF badge sewn on to the sleeve.

She noticed, and her posture straightened. Pride wasn't something Annie or any of the Hennessy women had in short supply.

"Why do you care?"

"Sweetheart was once my home."

"For two years." Her voice broke. "Then you left."

All this time, and she was obviously still hurting. Sam would give anything to change that.

"I came back for you."

"Not soon enough."

True. And he'd paid the price. So, apparently, had she. "We were young."

"That sounds like an excuse."

"I take responsibility for what happened between us, Annie. I'd say I wish things were different but then we wouldn't have our children. Neither of us would change that."

"You're right." Her stiff posture had yet to relax. "If you'll excuse me, it's time for me to head home."

"You're angry I bought the ranch. I get that."

"For starters."

He placed a hand on her arm, and then removed it when she glared at him. "Please, Annie. Help me help Sweetheart."

"What about your job in California?"

"My foreman is covering for me the rest of the summer.

Lyndsey and I will head home before school starts the first of September. After that, I'll fly here as often as needed. Lyndsey's grandfather will watch her."

Annie sucked in a sharp breath. Sam had hit a nerve.

After he'd left her that last time, he'd returned to California and within a matter of months wed his boss's daughter. Annie must have been devastated when the whole reason he'd accepted the job in the first place was because he wasn't ready for a commitment.

"I am sorry about your wife's death," she said.

"It was rough." Only Sam's father-in-law knew how rough. Sam would move heaven and earth to make sure Lyndsey never learned the entire circumstances of that terrible accident. "I'm in Sweetheart to start over and to get this town on its feet."

He couldn't tell her the real reason he was here, of his part in the fire or how often he'd thought of her during the past nine years. She'd never speak to him again.

"Why did you have to buy the Gold Nugget?" she asked.

"Ranching is my livelihood. What I know best." He intentionally omitted his volunteer firefighting. "And, honestly, I figured if you hadn't bought the Gold Nugget by now, you must have changed your mind."

"I didn't." Turning abruptly, she started toward her SUV.

"Annie, wait." He hurried after her.

She didn't stop until she was almost to the driver's door, and then not because of him. She'd spotted Lyndsey, who emerged from behind the house.

"Daddy," she called.

Sam could have kicked himself. He usually watched his daughter like a hawk. Today, he'd forgotten all about her. "Over here, sweetie."

"Look what I found in a hollow log behind the barn." She held the hem of her pink T-shirt out in front of her, the weight of whatever she carried making it dip in the middle.

Annie stood there frozen, observing Lyndsey's approach. He tried to imagine what she was thinking. Despite his daughter's girlish features, she resembled Sam, enough that most everyone who saw them together commented on it.

Not only had he married soon after that final parting with Annie, he'd fathered a child almost immediately. He wouldn't blame her if she hated him.

"What have you got?" Sam asked when Lyndsey neared.

The young girl eyed Annie with caution. Once outgoing and at ease with adults, she'd withdrawn since her mother's death. Leaving her home and friends and beloved grandfather behind for the summer hadn't helped, either. She'd been determined not to like Sweetheart from the moment Sam had announced they were going there.

"Lyndsey, this is Annie Hennessy," he said. "She's an old friend of mine from when I lived here."

Annie sent him a cool look, and he could almost hear her saying, *Old friend?*

When she focused her attention on his daughter, however, her expression melted. Annie did love children.

"Nice to meet you, Lyndsey."

Sam vowed in that moment he wouldn't leave Nevada until Annie looked at him with that same warmth.

Lyndsey responded with a shy "Hello."

"What have you got there?" Sam crossed the few steps separating them. When he saw what his daughter had cradled in her T-shirt, his heart sank. Lyndsey was going to be disappointed again, and he couldn't prevent it. "Oh, sweetie, I think they're dead."

"No, they're alive. See, they're moving." Gathering the hem of her shirt in a small fist, she tentatively touched one of the baby raccoons with her other hand. It moved slightly and gave a pitiful mew, rousing its littermate, which also mewed. "There were two other ones in the log, but they weren't…" She continued when she was more composed. "I left them there."

"I think you should put these two back in the log."

"But they'll die, too!"

"The mother can take care of them."

"The mother's gone." Lindsey's cheeks flushed the same pink shade as her T-shirt. "Something must have happened to her. Why else would she leave her babies?"

Sam wanted to drop to his knees and pull her into his arms. She was projecting her own unresolved emotions onto the situation. Wasn't that how the grief counselor had described her behavior during one of their sessions?

It was hardly the first time and wouldn't be the last. They both had a lot of healing left to do.

"Daddy." Her voice warbled. "We can't let them die."

"What would we do with two baby raccoons?"

"We can raise them. Until they're big enough to live by themselves. We read a story in school about this family that rescued baby animals after Hurricane Katrina."

"They're so tiny. I doubt they can even walk yet. We don't know the first thing about raising—"

"Kitten formula."

Sam glanced over at Annie. While he'd been talking to his daughter, she'd edged closer.

"Dr. Murry in town can help you. He'll set you up with bottles and formula. You'll need a box and a blanket and a lamp to keep them warm. He'll tell you more about that, too." She gently stroked the head of one baby raccoon with her index finger. "They're severely dehydrated. If you don't get fluids in them soon, they won't last."

"Have you raised baby raccoons before?" Lyndsey asked.

"A few. Along with kittens, puppies, squirrels, rabbits, snakes, a crow, you name it. There was even a fox once."

Sam knew the fox hadn't survived from the stories Annie told him.

"Wow." Lyndsey gaped at Annie with awe.

"My guess is these little fellows are about eight or nine

weeks old. And they would be walking if they weren't so weak. The mother might have had trouble finding food since the fire and wandered too far. If you're going to save them, you'd better get them to Doc Murry's right away. Anyone in town can direct you to his office."

"Lyndsey." Sam hated letting his daughter down, but he had to be realistic. "We're leaving in a month. Those raccoons won't be old enough to live on their own by then."

"Will you take care of them after that?" Lyndsey ignored Sam in favor of Annie.

"That's a lot to ask of Ms. Hennessy—"

"I'll figure something out," Annie assured Lindsey with a tender smile.

"You don't have to," Sam said.

"There's the wildlife refuge outside of Lake Tahoe. We're on a first-name basis. But you're going to have to save them first." She brushed Lyndsey's tousled hair from her face. "Better hurry. Keep them as quiet as possible during the ride."

"Come on, Daddy." Lyndsey started for the truck, wrapping an arm protectively around her precious cargo.

"Where are you staying?" Annie asked Sam.

"At the Mountainside Motel." The only one in Sweetheart open for business after the fire. "But we check out tomorrow. I have some furniture arriving. A few basics. Enough for Lyndsey and me to stay at the ranch."

"I'll try and stop by after work if I don't have to stay late. Just to check on the raccoons," she clarified when he raised his brows.

"Of course." He studied her closed-off expression. "Thank you."

"I didn't do it for *you*." She walked away then.

Sam watched her go. Same proud, stubborn Annie.

"Daddy! Hurry."

"Coming."

As they traveled the winding drive to the main road, a

smile spread across his face. Annie might refuse his assistance at every step, but together they were going to rebuild her inn.

He owed her that much at least.

Chapter Two

Sam Wyler was back!

Annie still hadn't come to grips with that fact twenty minutes later when she pulled into the parking space beside the Hennessy half of the duplex they rented in town.

She'd kept one eye glued to her rearview mirror during the entire drive from the Gold Nugget, hoping he hadn't followed her. The last thing she wanted was for him to see where she lived.

Not that the two-bedroom apartment was exactly trashy. Just small and modest and nothing compared with the lovely and charming suite of rooms she'd occupied at the inn. The rooms Sam had seen when they'd sneak off to be alone and make love.

She'd assumed those nights spent together would last forever. Then, he'd left, returned, left again and married—because the daughter of the rancher who hired him was carrying his child—and become a father.

Annie stayed behind in Sweetheart, hoping for the same future every couple who eloped here did. Only that happy ending had eluded her.

Mostly. As Sam had pointed out, she did have her beautiful little girl. For now, at least.

Her ex-husband had recently started hinting that he and his new wife could provide a better environment for Nessa than an eight-hundred-and-fifty-square-foot apartment shared by four individuals. What next? Would he go so far as to sue Annie for primary custody? She didn't think so, but everyone and everything had changed of late.

It was true, now that the inn had burned, that Gary could provide better for their daughter. And, marital differences aside, he'd always been a good father.

That made no difference to Annie. If he tried to obtain primary custody of their daughter, he and his new wife—Annie would lay odds Linda Lee was behind this—were in for the fight of their lives.

If only Sam hadn't suddenly reappeared, knocking Annie for an emotional loop. She didn't need anything distracting her from what mattered the most: rebuilding the inn and safeguarding her family.

She swung open the apartment door and stepped inside.

"Mommy! You're home." Nessa ran at her from across the living room like a miniature missile, her face smeared with some unidentifiable food remains and a Barbie doll with chopped-off hair clutched in her hand.

Annie scooped up her daughter and let herself feel truly good for the first time since leaving the apartment that morning.

"Hey, sweetums. How was your day?"

"Good. Grandma and I made biscuits. I ate two whole ones by myself. With jelly."

That explained the smeared food on Nessa's face. She tickled the girl's tummy. "How on earth did you put that much in there?"

"I'm big now."

"Yes, you are."

"You wanna play Barbies with me?"

"Maybe later. Mommy's a little tired."

"You're always tired," Nessa complained. "Ever since the fire. Grandma, too. And Great-granny Orla."

From the mouths of babes.

"I feel much better now that I'm home." She set Nessa down and kissed the tip of her nose, which was the only clean spot on her entire face.

"You want a biscuit and jelly? I can fix it for you."

"That'd be wonderful."

Annie sat on the couch and slowly removed her heavy hiking boots. By the end of the day, they felt as if they were lined with cement. She sighed when the first boot hit the floor, almost cried with relief when the second one followed.

Leaning back, she closed her eyes and relaxed for just a minute, listening to her mother patiently caution Nessa to be careful and not spill any jelly, in much the same way she'd cautioned Annie when she was growing up.

No one knew their way around the kitchen better than Fiona Hennessy. For almost her entire life, she'd overseen meals and housekeeping for the inn's twenty or thirty guests. Her small, compact stature belied the iron fist with which she'd ruled her domain.

These past six weeks, Fiona had continued the tradition of spending most of her time in the kitchen. Only now she was hiding from the world and desperately missing all that had been taken from her.

No more lion's claw bathtubs in the upstairs bedrooms, large enough to hold two. No more handmade, valentine-patterned quilts on which were strewn dried rose petals for arriving honeymooners. Or carved wooden trays that had held champagne breakfasts, discreetly delivered with a soft knock on the door. No more do-not-disturb signs, often hanging on doorknobs all the day long.

Annie hoped her mother's depression was temporary. More than that, she hoped her ex-husband, Gary, didn't notice Fiona's detachment when he picked up Nessa for "his days." That would only strengthen his argument that the apartment wasn't a good place to raise their daughter.

She would never wish him harm but often caught herself

wondering why fate had chosen the inn to burn and left Gary's house and place of business intact.

"Here you go, Mommy."

Opening her eyes, Annie was greeted by Nessa holding a paper plate with two jelly-laden biscuit halves.

"That looks good." Annie pushed tiredly to her feet. "Maybe I should eat it in the kitchen." She took the plate from Nessa, amazed the biscuit halves hadn't already landed on the carpet. "What else is for dinner?"

"Nothing," Nessa singsonged. "Just biscuits."

Uh-oh. Annie walked to the kitchen, her steps slow and her stomach sinking. Nessa danced in circles beside her. Fiona stood at the sink, staring vacantly out the window. Definitely not good.

Her mother watched Nessa during the day while Annie worked for the NDF. Her paycheck and Granny Orla's social security, which she'd started collecting just this month, were their only sources of income. Without them, they wouldn't be able to afford even this lowly apartment.

Lately, Annie had begun to question if her mother was up to the task of caring for an active child. More and more often, Fiona would disappear into her own world. For minutes on end. Five, ten, twenty. Long enough for an unsupervised Nessa to find trouble.

What Fiona should be doing while Nessa played was dealing with the insurance company, finalizing their settlement and obtaining quotes from contractors for rebuilding the inn. That was their agreement.

Hard to do when she could barely drag herself out of bed in the mornings.

"Where's Granny Orla?" Annie asked Nessa, hoping her question would rouse her mother. "Taking a nap?"

"I dunno."

"At the Rutherfords," Fiona answered without looking away from the window. "They called."

"How long has she been there?"

"Most of the afternoon, I guess."

The Rutherfords and the Hennessys' other neighbors were a godsend. Annie's grandmother, sharp as a tack until the fire, had started taking walkabouts during the day, easily escaping Fiona's less-than-diligent guard. She mostly wound up on some neighbor's doorstep—one whose house hadn't been lost to the fire. The neighbor would invite her inside until Annie came by later to fetch her.

Last week, Annie had found Granny Orla at the inn ruins and was shocked she'd managed the two-mile trek alone.

Annie doubted Alzheimer's or senility was responsible for her grandmother's increasing confusion. Like all of them, she'd suffered a great loss. And, also like them, she'd chosen a means of coping. Fiona emotionally retreated, Annie buried herself in work and Granny Orla chose to forget.

"I'll go get her." Annie set her plate of biscuits on the table, the little appetite she'd had now gone. "You want to come with me, sweetums?"

"Yes, yes!" Nessa swung her Barbie in an arc.

"Okay. But you have to pick up your toys and finish your milk first." Annie cringed inwardly. Biscuits and milk wasn't the most nutritious meal. Then again, Nessa wouldn't starve.

Annie should eat, too, if only to keep up her strength. Seeing Sam had drained the last of it.

Why had he chosen now to return, and why buy the Gold Nugget? She still couldn't believe he'd asked for her help.

While Nessa gathered the many toys strewn throughout the house and returned them to the plastic crate stored in the bedroom she and Annie shared, Annie changed into more-comfortable clothes.

"We shouldn't be long," she said upon returning to the kitchen.

Fiona, who hadn't moved from the window, suddenly turned and stared at Annie with more intensity than she'd shown in weeks. "Sam Wyler's in town. He bought the Gold Nugget."

That took Annie by surprise. "I know," she said. "How did you hear?"

"Everyone's talking about it."

"I ran into him. On my way home. I stopped by the Gold Nugget, and he was there."

"I suppose if someone had to buy the ranch, I'd rather it be him."

"Mom! How can you say that?"

Fiona went slowly to the table, pulled a chair out for herself and dropped into it. "He's one of our own."

"Because he lived here two years?" Annie was aghast at her mother's calm acceptance. "He's going to turn it into a working guest ranch."

"I'm not sure that's such a good idea."

Finally! Reason had returned. "I agree. A bed-and-breakfast makes more sense." Like her own plans for the place.

"I like the idea of a working guest ranch. Not sure why someone didn't think of that before."

"But you said—"

"What I meant was the fire's discouraged people from coming to Sweetheart. Bed-and-breakfast or working guest ranch, both need customers."

"Fine with me. When he flops, we'll buy the ranch from him."

"Sam was always a hard worker. If anyone can pull it off, he can." Fiona talked as if she hadn't heard Annie.

"He'll be in competition with us. Once we rebuild."

"If we rebuild," Fiona said tiredly.

Annie didn't listen to her mother when she got this way. "Did you have a chance to make Nessa's immunization appointment at the clinic?"

Fiona shook her head. "I was busy."

Biscuit making? Annie thought grouchily. Did that take all afternoon?

She tried to be patient and understanding with her mother. Really she did. Fiona's fragile emotional state made the task of rebuilding too overwhelming for her to bear. But once they broke ground, she and Annie's grandmother would be their old selves and life would return to normal.

Annie had to believe that. If not, she'd be overwhelmed herself, and she couldn't afford to let that happen.

Long before they finished rebuilding, however, Sam's working guest ranch would be up and running. Damn him! Annie wanted their inn and not Sam's ranch bringing the honeymooners and tourists back to Sweetheart.

"Mrs. Rutherford mentioned Sam has a little girl."

"He does." Annie made herself eat a biscuit half in case Nessa noticed.

Normally, her daughter would be pestering her to leave. Instead, she'd become interested in a puzzle she was supposed to be putting away.

"I heard she looks like him," Fiona said.

The food stuck in Annie's throat. "No need for DNA testing. She's Sam's child through and through."

Except for the sorrow in her eyes.

Annie was no psychiatrist, she didn't have to be. The girl was obviously troubled—which might not be Sam's fault. Her mother had died and, as Annie could attest, life-altering events changed a person.

"I bet he's a good dad."

She rose from the table, not wanting to talk about Sam or his daughter. "Come on, Nessa. Find your shoes so we can go get Granny Orla."

Nessa abandoned the puzzle and went on the hunt for her shoes.

"It was a shame things didn't work out for you and him,"

Fiona said from the table. "You must have really broken his heart."

"Let's not forget, he left me."

Fiona sighed. "Bound to happen. Can't fight the inevitable."

Her mother's words stayed with Annie as she and Nessa walked hand in hand to the Rutherfords'.

Ask anyone in town, and they'd say the Hennessy women were cursed. All of them, grandmother, mother and daughter, had loved their men, only to be abandoned by them. In Granny Orla and her mother's cases, they'd been left with a child to raise alone. Not Annie. Sam had simply taken off—which was practically unheard of in a town renowned for couples marrying.

Rather than be thought of as the third Hennessy woman to suffer unrequited love, Annie had rushed out and wed the first man to show an interest in her.

Can't fight the inevitable.

It hadn't made a difference. The Hennessy curse had continued with Annie. For here she was today, abandoned by not one but two men.

She squeezed Nessa's hand.

Please, please, she silently prayed, *don't let my baby be as unlucky in love as the rest of my family.*

SAM GAZED OVER AT LYNDSEY and mentally kicked himself. She—and he by default—were now foster parents to Porky Pig and Daffy Duck. Lyndsey had named their new charges while in Dr. Murry's office, after he informed her the pair were both males.

"Did you know baby raccoons are called kits?" Lyndsey struggled to buckle her seat belt while balancing the cardboard boot box containing the kits on her lap. Tube-fed, hydrated and vaccinated, they'd fallen into a deep sleep atop an old towel. "And when they get older, some people call them cubs."

"Is that so?"

Sam hadn't heard everything Dr. Murry told them and listened intently as Lindsey repeated the instructions. He'd received not one but two phone calls while at the vet's. The first from the moving company confirming the arrival of their furniture tomorrow. The second call was from a cattle broker regarding a shipment of calves.

Sam added hiring a livestock manager and locating a string of sound trail horses to his growing task list.

"Chicken's one of their favorite foods," Lyndsey said. "And sunflower seeds."

"Well, we should get along just fine as chicken and sunflower seeds are some of my favorite foods, too."

She giggled.

Giggled! Sam almost swerved off the road. He hadn't seen his daughter this happy since before her mother's accident.

Trisha Wyler had been pronounced dead upon arrival at the hospital after a drunk driver ran a stop sign and T-boned her Buick. Her passenger, on the other hand, lived long enough to confess Trisha's secret.

Sam didn't just lose his wife that day—his entire belief system was destroyed in one fell swoop.

His father-in-law was responsible for Sam keeping it together, reminding him daily of Lyndsey and the twenty employees at their three-thousand-acre cattle ranch who depended on him.

Sam went through the motions for six months, a huge, empty hole inside him that no amount of whiskey, angry rages, sympathy from friends and a seven-figure settlement could fill. Then, over a year ago, he returned to the Redding California Hotshots, a seasonal volunteer job he'd loved during the early years of his marriage. Within a few months, he was promoted to crew leader, then captain.

Long, grueling, sweat-filled days battling fires on the front line returned him to the world of the living.

Until the day the fire they were fighting in the Sierra Nevada Mountains jumped the ravine and bore down on the town of Sweetheart.

It was his fault. Had he disobeyed his commanding officer's orders like he wanted to, he might have saved the town. Saved Annie's family's inn. His superiors didn't hold him responsible but Sam did. Enough for ten people.

He quit the Hotshots a week later and found a real estate agent in Lake Tahoe who knew the Sweetheart area, his plan to return temporarily and assess how he could best help the town recover already in motion.

During one of their phone conversations, the agent mentioned the Gold Nugget Ranch. Sam made the offer the next day sight unseen and paid the full asking price without quibbling. As of tomorrow, he was officially in the hospitality business.

And, apparently, in the baby raccoon business, too. He'd foster a hundred of them if Lyndsey would only giggle again.

While Sam had immersed himself in wilderness firefighting as a means to conquer his grief, his daughter grew further and further apart from him. He hoped their time together in Sweetheart would remedy that. Still, one summer of being an attentive father couldn't wipe out eighteen months of neglect.

"We need to buy canned cat food," Lyndsey insisted. Her hand lay protectively on Porky and Daffy. "Dr. Murry said they're old enough for solid food."

Did baby raccoons bite? Sam couldn't remember the vet's advice. "We will."

"Tomorrow?"

He thought of his lengthening task list. What was one more item?

"Tomorrow. After the furniture arrives." He eased onto

the main road from the parking lot. It had grown dark outside while they were with the vet.

"How will we warm the milk?" Lyndsey asked.

"The stove works." If the propane tank was full and if he could locate a pan.

"Where will we get a cage?"

"The feed store might have one."

"What if they don't?"

"We'll figure something out. Don't worry." He could see his words had no effect. Worry lines creased his daughter's small brow.

Maybe he should call the grief counselor, get some advice on how to handle Lyndsey and her quickly forming attachment to the kits. Heaven knew he hadn't done well when left to his own devices.

"Ms. Hennessy might have a cage we can use." Was that still Annie's name or had she kept her ex-husband's?

Lyndsey's face lit up. "Do you think so?"

"Maybe."

Seriously? Who was he kidding? The inn had burned down to the ground. From what the real estate agent told him, Annie, her mother and grandmother were left with no more than a few hastily gathered personal possessions.

"Or, she might know someone who does," he suggested, thinking that possibility more likely.

"I want to take Porky and Daffy home to California with us," Lyndsey promptly announced.

"We already talked about this. You know it's not possible."

"Why not?"

"They're wild animals, not pets. Besides, you'll be busy with school."

"Benita will help me take care of them."

Their housekeeper barely tolerated dogs in the house. "Benita has enough to do."

"We can make a place for them in the backyard. Like at

the zoo. With a swimming pool and everything. Dr. Murry said raccoons like water."

What answer could he give that would make her understand?

"Lyndsey, we can't take them home. They belong here. In Sweetheart. Living free in the wild."

"But the woods are all burned and the animals ran away."

"The trees will grow back and the animals didn't all run away."

"They'll die like their mother and brothers!" Her voice quavered with outrage.

"We'll turn them over to someone who will take good care of them. Like the wildlife refuge Ms. Hennessy mentioned."

"I want to see it first." There was no arguing with her.

Well, she came by it honestly. If Sam wasn't so bullheaded, he might have realized his marriage was falling apart long ago and taken action—he had no idea *what* action.

"Fine. I promise. Wherever the baby raccoons go, you'll see the place first."

"Kits."

"Kits," he corrected himself, aware that round had gone to Lyndsey. "In the meantime, until we leave Sweetheart, you can keep them." He proceeded slowly through one of the town's two stoplights.

"I wanna call Grandpa and tell him about Porky and Daffy."

"When we get back to the mo—" Sam hit the brakes, checking the rearview mirror to make sure no one was close behind him.

Annie, her grandmother and a little girl that had to be her daughter were walking along the sidewalk. Annie appeared to be struggling for control. Orla Hennessy, all of seventy-five, if not eighty, went in one direction and the little girl in the other. Neither paid attention to Annie, who'd momentarily stumbled in the confusion.

What in the world were the three of them doing out after dark?

Pulling onto the side of the road, he beeped the horn, thrust the transmission into Park and depressed the emergency brake. "Lyndsey, wait here. Don't get out, you hear me?"

She sat up in her seat. "Where are you going?"

"To help Ms. Hennessy. I'll be right back."

She clasped the box to her as if Annie and her family were going to reach in and swoop up her prize possession. "We have to get Porky and Daffy back to the motel and feed them."

"This won't take long."

"Ask her if she has a cage."

Did she ever run out of questions?

"Hey, there." Sam darted around the front of the truck to the sidewalk. "Out for an evening stroll?"

"Walking back from a friend's house," came Annie's tight-lipped reply.

"Hop in, and I'll give you a lift."

"No, thanks. We're fine."

He was surrounded by stubborn women.

"Sam Wyler! As I live and breathe, is that you?" Granny Orla broke away from Annie's grasp and propelled herself at Sam. "Aren't you a sight for sore eyes."

Sam returned the older woman's hug, his throat surprisingly tight. "How are you, Granny Orla?"

She held him at arm's length, giving him a thorough once-over, her eyes alight. "My, my. Handsome as ever. That granddaughter of mine should have never let you go."

"I'm right here, Granny." With both arms free, Annie had been able to secure a firm hold on her squirming daughter. "I can hear everything you're saying."

Granny winked at Sam. "I know that."

He flashed a broad grin in return. "I always did like you."

"That goes both ways, young man."

The older woman barely reached the middle of his chest. As Sam recalled, neither did Fiona Hennessy. Annie must have gotten her height from her father, whom she hadn't seen since starting first grade.

"You're a cowboy!"

Sam's attention was drawn downward to Annie's little girl, a tiny imp who more closely resembled her grandmother and great-grandmother than Annie. Except for her compelling green eyes, which were the same shape and color as her mother's.

"I am."

"Do you have a horse?" She studied him with suspicion, as if having a horse was the measure of a real cowboy.

"Lots of them, actually. At my ranch in California. And a pony. From when my daughter, Lyndsey, was your age."

"Can I ride him?"

"Nessa!" Annie gently chided the girl. "That's not polite."

"'Fraid California's too far away." Sam laughed, not the least offended. "But that's a good idea. I should have the pony shipped out here for the Gold Nugget. Then your mom can bring you over for a ride."

"What's the pony's name?"

He surveyed the traffic, which was light but a potential danger nonetheless. "Get in, and I'll tell you about her on the drive home."

"Can we, Mommy? Please?" Nessa yanked on Annie's arm, stretching it to its limit.

Granny Orla was one step ahead of her great-granddaughter. "Fine idea."

Outnumbered and clearly at her wits' end, Annie sighed resignedly.

Sam allowed himself a grin as he opened the rear passenger door and helped the three inside. Annie didn't avail herself of the hand he offered, but he didn't let that deter him.

He had the opportunity of sharing her company for the next several minutes and intended to make full use of it.

Chapter Three

Sam's daughter twisted around in the front seat the second Annie got into the truck.

"Did my dad ask you about a cage for the kits?"

"Just a minute ago." She tried not to be swayed by the blaze of hope shining in the girl's face. "I'll get one for you by tomorrow and drop it off."

"Really? Thank you!"

So much for not being swayed.

"What are kits?" Nessa asked, unable to sit still.

"Baby raccoons," Lyndsey answered.

"Where? Can I see?" She leaned forward.

"When we stop the truck, if you're good." Annie placed a restraining hand on her daughter.

"We'll be at the ranch tomorrow early," Sam said. "The furniture truck's due."

Great. She was now going to visit Sam a *second* time at the Gold Nugget, *and* he was taking her home. What else could go wrong?

"Mind if I tag along?" her grandmother asked.

"You're welcome anytime."

"It won't be till later, Granny. I'll be coming straight from work, not stopping home first."

"Haven't seen the place in a while," her grandmother continued as if she hadn't heard Annie. "Not since last spring."

"I wanna go, too," Nessa chimed in.

Annie should have silenced her thoughts when she had the chance. At least Nessa seemed to have forgotten about the pony. For now.

"How are you getting along, Granny Orla?" Sam slowed, taking the turn leading to Annie's street. She'd given him directions when they first climbed into the truck.

"Terrible." Her grandmother went from animated to forlorn in the span of a single second. "We lost the inn."

"I heard. I'm sorry."

"Not half as sorry as I am. Don't know how we're going to make it. Much less rebuild."

"We'll find a way. Don't worry." Annie's assurance was as much for herself as everyone else in the truck. Especially Nessa. She might not understand everything they were going through, but she was astute and picked up on people's moods.

"I told Annie I'd like to help with rebuilding Sweetheart." Sam parked in front of the duplex. "Your inn and the entire town."

"We're fine." Annie noticed his gaze traveling to the modest duplex. Grabbing her daughter's hand, she wrenched open the door. "Come on, Nessa." They were out in a flash.

"I want to see the kits."

"Later, okay? It's getting late and the kits are sleeping."

"But we forgot Granny Orla."

Nessa was right. Annie's grandmother hadn't moved.

"Come on, Granny. Mom's waiting for us."

"She is?"

"Yes."

"Where?"

"In the apartment."

"The apartment?" her grandmother repeated slowly. "What's she doing there?"

Why now? Annie silently lamented. And why in front of

Sam? She should have seen this coming. Any discussion about losing the inn brought on these...these...episodes.

"Please, Granny. It's getting late."

Sam came around the truck to the passenger side. "How 'bout I walk you to the door?"

The sympathy in his voice hit Annie hard. Half of her wanted to scream in frustration, the other half cry.

Nessa tugged on her hand. "Mommy, I have to go potty."

"Okay, just a second." Moving aside, Annie let Sam reach into the truck cab and coax her grandmother out.

Some of the older woman's animation returned. "Can't remember the last time a man walked me to my door."

"Wait here, Lyndsey," he instructed his daughter.

"The kits woke up. We have to feed them," she protested.

Annie could hear their soft mewing.

"I'll only be a minute," Sam said. "They won't starve."

Lyndsey slouched and hugged the box on her lap, her lower lip protruding.

Though it wasn't Annie's fault, she felt responsible for the delay. "I'll see you tomorrow, Lyndsey. When I bring the cage." She made a mental note to remember. "Will the kits be all right till then?"

"Dr. Murry showed me what I need to do." Her hand reached tenderly into the box.

Annie had no doubt Lyndsey would make the vet proud. If only her father had shown half that much tenderness when handling Annie's heart.

He did seem to be doing an admirable job with her grandmother, though. Was it possible he'd changed?

The front door swung open before Annie could dig her keys out of her pocket.

"There you are. I was getting worried." At the sight of Sam, Fiona's depression evaporated. "Sam Wyler!"

Annie's mother hugged him fiercely, much as her grandmother had. The gesture made Annie acutely aware that she and Sam had yet to touch since his return.

"How are you?" Fiona asked. "Come in, come in."

Annie ground her teeth. *Say no. Please.*

For once, her luck held.

"Thank you, Fiona, but I can't." He straightened his cowboy hat, which had been knocked askew during the hug. "My daughter's waiting in the truck."

"Bring her in, too. We'll have some ice cream."

"Ice cream!" Nessa jumped up and down.

"I appreciate the offer." Sam shot a look at the truck parked on the curb. "But Lyndsey's babysitting a pair of abandoned raccoons she found earlier today in a log, and they need feeding."

"Raccoons?"

"Annie can explain."

"Then you'll have to come back another day. Your daughter, too."

"I'd like that."

"I'm gonna ride a pony," Nessa chimed in, forgetting all about her pressing need. "You said I could."

Sam patted her head. "I have to buy some horses first."

"High Country Outfitters are going out of business," Fiona said, "and selling off their entire stable of trail horses. With no customers, they can't afford the price of feed. You could probably pick up a few good head for a decent price."

"Who do I talk to?"

"Will Dessaro's their livestock manager. Anyone in town can tell you where to find him."

"I'll track him down first thing in the morning."

Annie almost did a double take. How was it her mother knew about High Country Outfitters going out of business and she'd heard nothing?

Because she'd been busy with work and caring for Nessa and holding her family together.

And she hadn't wanted to know. With each resident that was forced to move from Sweetheart, each business that shut its doors, she lost a small sliver of hope.

"I'd best get going, see to it those raccoons get fed." Sam touched the brim of his hat and grinned at all of them. Annie the longest.

Her heart might be damaged, but it could still flutter. Which, to her dismay, it did.

If only Sweetheart were bigger than three square miles and one thousand residents—a number dwindling daily. Then maybe she wouldn't be constantly running into Sam.

As she watched him stride confidently toward his truck, she wondered if that wasn't what she secretly wanted. She had, after all, made an excuse to see him tomorrow.

She spun on her heels to find her mother, grandmother and daughter all watching him, too.

Apparently she wasn't the only one susceptible to his charms.

THE PICKUP AND STOCK TRAILER looked out of place as it rumbled to a stop beside the old corral. So did the modern furniture that had been delivered hours earlier and set up in the ranch's three bedrooms, kitchen and parlor.

Sam's memories of the Gold Nugget were of a buggy sitting in front of the house, knotty pine rockers on the porch, blacksmith equipment hanging in the shed beside the barn and rooms filled with antiques and authentic reproductions used in filming *The Forty-Niners*. There had also been photographs of the stars and crew displayed on every wall in every room, along with articles on the actors' lives and trivia about the show.

For some unknown reason, those photos alone had survived when everything else in the house was auctioned off.

In the evenings, after the tourists had left, the ranch would become eerily quiet. He and Annie would sit in the rockers or at the long oak table in the kitchen or lie on the squeaky mattress and box spring in the master bedroom and dream about the future.

If old Mrs. Litey, the longtime curator of the Gold Nugget, had caught them, she'd have skinned them alive.

And now, the ranch was Sam's, thanks to the former owner deciding it was easier to sell the place than make the necessary repairs and upgrades.

A quick glance around revealed the ranch still needed a lot of work—starting with the corrals. The pine rails were broken and rotted in place and wouldn't contain the horses he'd purchased that morning for very long. Fortunately, the construction contractor and his crew were arriving on Monday.

Sam walked over to greet the young cowboy emerging from the cab of the truck, a large shepherd mix tumbling out after him. Sam and Will Dessaro had spent a good two hours together, during which Sam inspected each horse in the High Country Outfitters' string and negotiated the price. The deal was closed when he delivered the cashier's check he'd obtained at the neighboring town fifteen miles away.

"You made good time." He shook Will's hand. The man's grip was firm, his features strong and appealing. "Thought you might have some trouble loading all these horses by yourself."

"Not likely."

"Should we back the trailer up to the gate?" he asked.

"Don't need to."

This would be interesting, Sam thought as he watched Will open the rear of the trailer and lower the ramp. Only then did Sam realize all the horses stood loose, except for the first one. He alone was haltered and tied.

"Don't you think you should—"

Before Sam finished his thought, Will was leading the haltered horse down the ramp. The nine others followed out of the trailer, one by one, nose to tail. The dog trotted along beside them. To Sam's surprise, all ten horses stood quietly as Will opened the corral gate and then pushed inside, eagerly exploring their new home. Will swung the gate shut and latched it.

"I'm impressed," Sam said.

"Not a contrary one in the bunch."

Sam was a believer and convinced he'd made a good investment.

Together, he and Will unloaded bags of feed from the trailer's front compartment and stacked them under the lean-to. Next, they ran a hose and filled the water barrel.

"Be back in an hour with the rest of them." Will had promised he could deliver all nineteen horses in two trips, and it looked as though he was a man of his word.

"Any chance you can stick around afterward and maybe tomorrow? Help me with the horses?"

"Sure."

"I'm not interfering with your job?"

"High Country Outfitters is out of business. You just bought what was left of my job."

"Sorry about that."

Will shrugged. "I noticed some of the horses have loose shoes."

"Is there a farrier in town?"

"I did most of the shoeing for High Country."

"Any experience with cattle?"

"My grandmother raised me. She ran near a hundred head."

Will was looking better and better by the minute. He also knew the mountain trails.

"You're not by chance good at cross-country skiing?"

"Have all my own gear."

Well, well. "Anything you can't do?"

"Cook."

That made two of them. Lyndsey had already complained about breakfast and lunch.

Sam pushed his hat back and grinned. "You by chance in the market for a new job?"

"You offering me one?"

"I need a livestock foreman and someone to supervise the trail rides. Take guests on guided skiing excursions in the winter months. I'm thinking you have the experience."

"Okay." Will started toward his truck. His dog, resting in the shade of a bush, sprang instantly to its feet.

"Is that a yes?" Sam called after him.

"You need something in writing?"

He laughed. "We'll talk details when you get back."

"Fine by me."

Sam decided he liked the Gold Nugget Ranch's first official employee. The female guests were bound to like him, too, though Sam suspected Will would keep to himself.

Pressed for time, Sam went over to the corral and checked on the horses. Several bunched at the railing for a petting. The rest stared at him as if wondering why they hadn't been given any pellets.

"When your buddies arrive." He patted an overly eager black-and-white paint that could easily break through the railing if he weren't so docile. "And when I figure out what exactly I'm going to use for a feed trough."

By all accounts, there'd been no horses on the ranch since *The Forty-Niners* ceased production. He'd considered himself lucky to find that old water barrel in the barn.

There must be something else kicking around he could use. If not, he'd ask Will. The man struck Sam as being the resourceful type. And there was always the feed store.

He was halfway to the barn when a rusted-out sedan pulled into the ranch and stopped, the exhaust spewing a cloud of gray smoke when the engine was cut. Seconds later, a woman with an assortment of children spilled out of all four doors.

"Hi, can I help you?"

"Mr. Wyler? My name's Irma Swichtenberg. These here are my children."

The tallest, a teenager, tugged nervously on her hair while the shortest, a toddler, snuggled a stuffed toy.

"What can I do for you?" Sam asked.

"Miss Hennessy sent me your way."

"Annie?"

"No, sir. Fiona. I worked for her. At the inn. Housekeeping. She said you might be looking to hire someone." The woman swallowed nervously. "I'm a hard worker. Honest and dependable. Carrie watches the little ones for me so I won't ever miss a day." She placed a hand on the teenager's shoulder.

Sam could see Irma Swichtenberg was a proud woman and that asking for a job didn't come easy. For all he knew, she single-handedly supported her small family. Judging by the shape of their worn clothes, she was at the end of her resources.

"How good a cook are you?"

"Passable."

"The place needs a lot of cleaning. Been empty awhile. And I'm hardly the neatest person. My daughter's worse."

"Not much I can't handle or won't."

He believed her.

"I really need a job, Mr. Wyler. I'll work cheap."

Sam had made a promise to himself to help the people of Sweetheart and that included providing employment for as many of the locals as possible. That aside, he'd have hired Irma anyway. He liked and respected her that much.

"No need to work cheap. I'll pay you a decent wage."

When he named the rate, Irma's hands flew to her mouth. "You're not joshing me, are you?"

"Can you start in the morning? 8:00 a.m."

"I'll start now!"

"That's not necessary." He chuckled. "We'll decide on your

schedule tomorrow. Might only be part-time until we're ready for guests."

"Thank you, Mr. Wyler." She rushed toward him, grabbed his hand and pumped it enthusiastically. "I'm grateful to you."

"My daughter and I are the ones who are grateful to you. Otherwise, we might starve or be buried alive in a mountain of dirty clothes."

She smiled shyly, displaying slightly crooked teeth. "I'll see you at eight sharp."

Something told him Irma would be here at seven forty-five. "Looking forward to it."

Gathering her brood, she hurried them to the car as if afraid Sam might change his mind.

Unlikely, he decided. So far, he was more than pleased with his staff. And he had Fiona Hennessy to thank.

If she and Annie weren't so determined to rebuild the inn, he'd hire Fiona to manage the Gold Nugget. He needed someone trustworthy, competent and with her vast hospitality experience. Someone whose skills would allow him to be a long-distance owner.

Sam made his way toward the barn in search of Lyndsey. She'd been in there the entire time with Porky and Daffy. A few good meals had made all the difference to the kits. They were active and curious and had already figured out their long, sharp claws were perfect tools for scaling the sides of a cardboard box.

They were also kind of cute, Sam had to admit, with their little button noses, whiskers and black face masks.

Lyndsey had moved them into an old wooden crate until the cage arrived. She couldn't be a more attentive and devoted caretaker. Sam was proud of her. And worried. He tried not to think about how she'd take losing the kits when the time came.

She was just where he'd left her, sitting cross-legged in the center of the barn floor. Sunlight poured in through cracks in the wooden walls, painting a pattern of stripes on her and the crate beside her.

"Hi, Dad." She cradled Daffy, the smaller of the kits, in her lap, his front paws balanced on her towel-covered forearm in the manner the vet had instructed. Daffy lustily drained a bottle of kitten formula.

"How're they doing?" Sam asked.

"They like the canned cat food!" Her face radiated delight. "Dr. Murry says they'll eat almost anything."

"They licked it off a spoon."

Sam's earlier concern returned. "They didn't bite you, did they?"

"Oh, Dad."

He took that as a no and breathed easier.

"Grandpa said he can't wait to see them."

"Lyndsey, sweetie." He reached for her. "You—"

She stiffened and pulled away. "Don't say we can't take them home."

"Okay, I won't."

Withdrawing his hand, he squatted beside the crate and gave Daffy a little scratch. Porky was attempting to squeeze his apple-shaped head between the narrow openings in the crate.

"I can't believe how much difference one day makes."

"Porky purred and kneaded my arm when he ate."

"No fooling?" Sam attempted to pet Porky. The kit jerked instantly back and growled at him, his fur standing on end. He looked and sounded more comical than threatening.

"Dad! Be careful. You'll hurt him."

"Hurt him? What about me?" Sam inspected his hand. "I'm the one who almost lost a finger."

"It's instinctive. You have to move slowly."

He turned at the sound of Annie's voice.

She stood in the entrance to the barn, wearing her NDF uniform and holding an empty cage.

"Hey. Thanks for coming by." He pushed to his feet, noticing the exhaustion on her face. "You okay?"

"Just beat. We ran erosion and water repellency tests all day in the field."

Despite her busy schedule, she'd found time to locate a cage for Lyndsey and deliver it. If he could, he would take her in his arms and the hell with the consequences.

"Sounds grueling."

"It was."

She must have seen the urge reflected in his eyes because she retreated a step—just like she'd done yesterday when they first met and again last night when he picked her up on the way home.

Would she ever stop being wary of him? And if she did, what then?

Nothing, he thought. Even if they were able to move past their unhappy history, the timing was off, for both of them, and no amount of wishing would change that.

Chapter Four

Annie tried not to stare at Sam as she set the cage down and walked over to Lyndsey. He didn't make it easy. Levi's, a faded chambray shirt and a Stetson covering thick, dark hair in need of a cut was a look he wore well.

Standing straight, she reminded herself he'd left her high and dry. Not once, but twice. There would be no third time.

"Gosh, would you look at them!" She directed her smile at Lyndsey and the kits.

"They're eating canned cat food!" Lyndsey exclaimed. One kit scrambled up her chest toward her shoulder while the other one clawed at the crate.

"Already? I'm impressed."

"You think they're going to be all right?"

The kits were active, alert and responsive. All encouraging signs.

"It's a little too soon to say for certain, but my guess is they'll make it."

"Why did their mommy and brothers die? Was it because of the fire?"

"Not the fire itself." Annie started to say the entire eco-structure in the area had been profoundly altered, which, in turn, affected local wildlife, then decided the explanation was too complicated for an eight-year-old. "The land's changed, and the animals are have a harder time surviving than they once did."

"This one is Daffy." Lindsey lifted the kit from her lap into the air. "Want to hold him?"

"Sure." Annie took the kit and cradled it close. The warm feel and musky scent were familiar. How many baby raccoons had she rescued and raised? Six? Ten?

Now she was rescuing and raising her family. If only that were as easy as a pair of kits.

"You'd better take him." She returned Daffy to Lyndsey. "The fewer people who handle him and his brother, the better."

"Why?"

"They'll adjust easier to the animal sanctuary or the wild."

Lyndsey sucked in a gasp. "Won't they just die if you let them go?"

"At this age, yes. But the sanctuary will care for them until they're old enough to be safely released. And they'll teach them how to find food and to take care of themselves."

"That's what Ms. Hennessy did." The remark came from Sam. "With all the animals she took in."

"Some. Others weren't ever able to fend for themselves."

"What happened to them?" Lyndsey hugged Daffy closer.

"I kept them for the rest of their lives."

"You had quite a collection," Sam said. "I'd help you feed and clean the enclosures." He looked at Lyndsey. "Her mother used to call it the zoo."

Annie snuck a quick peek at him. The thrill she'd fended off earlier wound through her, proving she wasn't immune to him and the easy, sexy charm he exuded.

As if she'd ever been.

He was older now. Experience had left its mark on his face and made him even more handsome—and her more susceptible.

"Wow!" Lyndsey's eyes went wide. "That must have been cool."

"It was," Sam concurred. "And then, she'd treat my horses whenever they needed some minor medical attention. Cuts, colic, vaccinations. We were a good team." His gaze found hers and held it.

"Once, maybe." A rush of memories assailed Annie, and she forced herself to look away.

"You're like a vet!"

Thankfully, Lyndsey appeared unaware of the emotions flying between Annie and her father.

"Not hardly. But I thought I wanted to be one when I was your age."

"What stopped you?" Sam asked.

She turned and faced him. "The inn. I was needed there."

"Do you ever regret your choice?"

"Not for one second. Sweetheart Inn has been in my family for three generations. It will be for a fourth."

"What happened to the animals?" Lyndsey asked.

"I stopped collecting so many after your dad…after a while." Annie went over and retrieved the cage from where she'd left it. "Where are you keeping the kits?"

"In my bedroom," Lyndsey promptly answered.

"That was just for last night." Sam bent and stroked her hair. "We talked about this. The barn is the best place."

She pulled away, her mouth set in a firm line. "You always say no."

Annie sensed the friction between them wasn't due entirely to the kits. This battle had been waged before over something else.

"Your dad's right," she said gently. "The barn is better. For one thing, unless you clean their cage ten times a day, they'll smell. Really bad."

"I'll clean it."

"And they're noisy. Raccoons are mostly nocturnal."

"Nocturnal?"

"They sleep during the day and are awake at night. They'll keep you up and everyone else in the house."

"I'll sleep during the day." Lyndsey put the kit back into the crate. He and his brother immediately began play fighting, tussling and growling at each other.

"Sweetie," Sam said, his patience showing signs of wearing thin, "you can't."

Annie had anticipated Lyndsey's objection even before her father finished speaking.

"Why!" She sprang to her feet, fists clenched at her sides. "I'm not in school or summer camp." She wrenched away when he reached for her. "You won't let me do anything."

Annie should just shut up. She had more than enough of her own problems to deal with without involving herself in Sam's. Yet, she couldn't stop herself.

"You could sleep out here with the kits."

Lyndsey stopped and gaped first at Annie, then Sam. "Can I, Daddy?"

"I don't think that's a good idea."

"Why not?"

"We don't have a cot, for one thing."

"Lay a tarp down next to the cage," Annie suggested. "Put a sleeping bag or some blankets on top of it."

"I don't want Lyndsey sleeping in the barn. It's not safe." His tone implied Annie might be interfering.

She should quit while she was ahead. Only, she didn't. "You could sleep out here with her."

Lyndsey jumped up. "Please, Daddy?"

"We'll see." He was clearly not enthused.

"Thank you, thank you." Lyndsey took his hedging as a yes and hugged him hard, pressing her face into his shirtfront.

He hugged her in return, his hand splayed protectively across her small back. The tender exchange charmed Annie.

Damn Sam. He was always getting to her. And now he'd

added his cute, sweet and obviously wounded daughter to his arsenal.

"Come on, kiddo. Let's get the cage set up." Annie kept her voice matter-of-fact.

The three of them worked for the next twenty minutes, during which time Annie continued instructing Lyndsey on baby raccoon care. They covered such topics as water for drinking and bathing, diet—the kits would benefit from natural foods like fruit and nuts—and how best to clean the cage without them escaping.

Lyndsey was an apt student, but Annie was aware that Sam spent more time watching her than the kits, causing the back of her neck to heat uncomfortably beneath her uniform collar. Was he still annoyed at her for suggesting he and Lyndsey sleep in the barn?

"I have to run," she said when the cage was secured atop some wooden blocks and fully equipped with everything the kits would need, including an old stuffed toy of Nessa's that Annie found in the SUV.

Lyndsey flung herself at Annie, and she instinctively held the girl. Sam was a lucky man. She only hoped he realized it.

"Thanks for everything," he said. Without asking, he accompanied her outside.

"It's the least I can do. By some miracle those kits survived when few other animals in these woods have."

"You really think Lyndsey will be okay in the barn?"

"Look, I shouldn't have said anything earlier. It wasn't my place."

"I'm not angry."

"Honestly, I'll be surprised if she lasts the entire night. She'll probably wake you up about midnight, wanting to go inside."

"Don't tell me. You've spent the night with baby raccoons before." Amusement lit his eyes.

"Guilty. I was just like Lyndsey and didn't take my

mother's advice." She paused at the SUV's door. "Can I make another suggestion without overstepping?"

"Sure." He leaned against the hood, crossing his arms and one boot over the other in a sexy stance that was very reminiscent of their younger days.

There'd been a time when she would have leaned against the hood beside him, assuming her own sexy stance.

"Buy Lyndsey a book on raising kits," she said, focusing her attention on the barn. Anywhere but on Sam.

"Do they sell those in the feed store?"

"If not, order one online or print out articles from the internet."

"I don't know." His brow furrowed. "She's getting pretty attached to the critters as it is. Learning more about them might make it harder to give them up."

"Or easier. But that's not the point."

He gazed at her with interest. "What is?"

And here she was giving him credit for trying to be an attentive father. "If you have to ask, there's no use in me explaining."

"I'm a bit denser than most."

She huffed. "Spending time with your daughter. Supporting her interests."

"Like I used to do with yours."

His grin disarmed her for several seconds, during which a pickup truck and trailer pulled onto the grounds and made its way toward the corrals. Annie recognized the rig and the driver. She also noticed a group of horses she'd missed earlier, milling about in the corral.

"You bought High Country Outfitters' string."

Sam nodded, clearly pleased. "I'm also having Lyndsey's old pony and a few other seasoned work horses from California shipped out."

"That ought to get you started."

He didn't make a move to help Will unload the new arrivals. Then again, Will didn't require help.

"I hired Will, too. Oh, and Irma Swichtenberg."

"You hired our housekeeper?" Annie spun so fast the open SUV door caught her in the back.

"Your mother sent her by."

"My mother!" It couldn't be true. Sam was mistaken. "Why would she do that?"

"Irma needed a job."

"She has one with us."

"Even if you rebuild the inn, it'll take months. Irma can't wait that long."

Annie heard only one thing. "*If* I rebuild the inn?"

"All right, when. But in the meantime, you have to be realistic. Irma needs to work. She has a lot of kids depending on her."

"I am being realistic. I'm probably the most realistic person here."

His brows formed a deep V. "And I'm not?"

"A guest ranch? Seriously? This town is dying a slow death. No one wants to come here and they won't, not until the forest regrows. And that could take decades."

"So, why rebuild the inn?"

Anger rushed in, filling the gaping hole left by his careless remark. "The Sweetheart Inn has been in my family for over fifty years. It's the heart of Sweetheart."

"I understand that."

"I thought you did," she retorted. "Now I'm not sure."

"As soon as you've finished construction, you can hire her back."

His conciliatory tone didn't assuage her. "She'll come, too. She's loyal to us."

"Nothing I'd like more than for you to rehire all your former employees."

That threw her for a loop. "Aren't you afraid of the competition?"

"No."

His lack of concern only made Annie angrier. "Because you think we can't do it."

"Because there's room in Sweetheart for two hospitality establishments. Besides—" his grin widened "—there isn't anyone I'd rather be in competition with than you."

He was absolutely infuriating.

She climbed in the SUV and drove away before he could disarm her yet again and undermine the really good mad she'd worked up.

"When was the deductible raised?"

"Last year, on your renewal."

Annie stared at the policy summary page, the renewal date in the corner and the deductible amount referenced in bold. Everything the insurance adjuster said was true.

"Mom?"

Fiona didn't reply. As usual, she was standing at the kitchen sink, gazing out the window—and had been during most of the meeting with the insurance adjuster. Sometimes, when asked a question, she'd answer. Sometimes not.

Annie's frustration reached a new level, outweighed only by her discouragement. Insurance wasn't her area of expertise—her mother handled it. Added to that, Annie had taken the afternoon off work, without pay, in order to participate in the meeting. The least her mother could do was cooperate.

"Mom!" she repeated.

Silence.

It had been like this for the past three days, since Annie came home from seeing Sam and questioned her mother's disloyalty.

Granted, *disloyalty* was too strong of a word, and she'd apologized for it later. But she'd been hurt and blindsided.

Irma needed a job, and her mother was right to refer her to a prospective employer. That Sam was the employer stung.

"A five-thousand-dollar deductible isn't uncommon." The adjuster, a portly middle-aged man, sat next to Annie at the kitchen table. He was kind and understanding and patient when it came to explaining the policy. Still, that didn't change the fact the Hennessys would have considerably more out-of-pocket expenses than Annie had anticipated.

"Most of the furnishings and household items were antiques. I don't understand why we're only getting fifty thousand dollars when they're worth more like a hundred thousand."

"That's how the policy was written."

Annie glanced at her mother. If Fiona noticed, she gave no indication.

Before the adjuster had arrived, and while Nessa was napping, they'd scratched out a rough estimation of what it would cost to rebuild, restock and refurnish the inn. The final number had staggered them both.

According to the adjuster, the insurance company would only compensate them for a little more than half that amount. Even more discouraging, according to the adjuster, their previous policy limits would have resulted in a considerably larger payout. But Annie's mother, in an effort to curb expenses in a recessed economy, had kept their premium payment affordable by raising the deductible and lowering the limits of their coverage.

She should have paid more attention when her mother mentioned her plan, making this partially her own fault. Instead, she'd gone about managing the inn's daily operations, leaving the business end and food service to Fiona.

It was an arrangement that had worked successfully for the past decade and would have continued working if not for a fire ravaging the town and turning the inn into a giant cinder box.

"I'm sorry," Fiona muttered, finally breaking the silence.

"It's all right, Mom. You did what you thought was right." Annie vowed that when they rebuilt, she'd insist they not skimp where insurance was concerned. "We'll figure out something."

What that something was, Annie didn't know yet. She'd drained a large part of their rainy-day fund for the cleaning and security deposits on their apartment and putting food on the table.

"There are some federal programs out there for people who qualify," the adjuster said.

Her mother was supposed to be looking into those. Annie didn't think there had been any progress, though. "That's our next step."

"It's a paperwork nightmare," Fiona added.

"But possibly well worth it." The adjuster removed his glasses and rubbed his eyes. He was obviously tiring and wanted Annie and her mother to sign off on the settlement agreement. "Maybe there are some areas you can trim."

Trimming is what had landed them in this jam to begin with. "We haven't actually received any quotes yet." Annie kneaded a crick in her neck. She was also growing tried—of the meeting and her mother's procrastination.

"What about your architect? He can design the inn with your budget in mind. Perhaps make it smaller."

"That's probably what we'll end up doing. When we hire an architect."

They could always add onto the inn later. As the town and the forests came back, so would the Sweetheart Inn. Annie preferred that to happen much faster, but they could take their time if needed. Just not too much time, she hoped.

"I understand there's a man in town," the adjuster said. "A Sam Wyler."

"What does he have to do with anything?"

"He brought in a construction contractor to remodel the Gold Nugget Ranch."

"So I heard," Annie said. Her mother's grapevine had reported that Sam's construction contractor and his crew had arrived yesterday.

"He's offering the services of the contracting crew to anyone in town who wants to use them and agreed to pick up a portion of the fee."

"Is that true?" Annie directed the question at her mother.

"So Hilda says."

Mayor Dempsey was a reliable source.

"It's true," the adjustor confirmed. "I have several other customers in town, and they've all told me the same. Haven't met the man, but it seems legit."

"Why would he agree to cover some of the contractor's costs?"

"Apparently he wants to help the town rebuild."

Exactly what he'd told Annie. "Where would he get that kind of money?"

She assumed Sam had done well for himself, given the new truck he drove and his ability to purchase the Gold Nugget, even at a reduced price. But money of the quantity they were talking about seemed vast even for him.

"I have no idea." The adjuster gathered the papers spread across the kitchen table and arranged them into a tidy stack.

"He was awarded a large settlement," Fiona said. "After his wife's accident."

More gossip from Mayor Dempsey. She made a point of keeping Annie's mother informed by calling regularly.

"Why would he spend the settlement money on Sweetheart?" It made no sense to Annie. "What about his daughter?"

"You might talk to him." The adjuster paused. "Seeing as you and he are acquainted."

Annie held her tongue, though it wasn't easy. The adjuster's other customers were probably delighted to spill the torrid details of Annie and Sam's former romance. The man probably knew everything there was about all three Hennessy women.

She shoved the insurance papers aside. Hell would freeze over before she approached Sam with a plea for assistance.

The insurance adjuster slid the settlement agreement back toward her. "This is probably the best you're going to get from the carrier. I recommend you—"

"I'm not ready to settle yet." She had been, until the man mentioned Sam.

"Ms. Hennessy—"

"No." Annie rose from the table. "I want more time. You said we have a few weeks."

"That you do." The adjuster stuffed the papers into his briefcase, minus the set for her. "Call me anytime."

Annie closed the front door after seeing the man off, a headache making its presence known. What she really wanted was to find her daughter and hold her. Kissing Nessa's sweet button nose and dimpled cheeks would restore her sagging spirits.

In the kitchen, Fiona had moved from the window. "Annie. Maybe we should reconsider. Accept the settlement."

Her mother had a point. "Moving ahead with the construction would do us all good."

"We don't have to rebuild."

That had to be the depression talking. Fiona wanted the inn as much as Annie and Granny Orla. "Of course we're going to rebuild. What else would we do?"

Fiona nodded. "I guess you're right." She started washing dishes.

Annie, more determined than ever, went in search of Nessa. There would be a new Sweetheart Inn. Maybe smaller to start with, but it would still be the heart of the town.

There had to be a new inn. If not, she and her family might never return to normal, and Annie couldn't let that happen.

Chapter Five

Nessa was in the bedroom she and Annie shared, sitting on the double bed beside Granny Orla. They had been more or less watching each other while Annie and her mother met with the insurance adjuster.

"What are you two doing?" She went over to Nessa, seeking the touch she needed and feeling restored.

"Playing." Nessa giggled giddily and uncovered what lay hidden beneath her collection of stuffed toys and Barbie dolls.

Laid out on the quilt were the different items Annie had salvaged from the ruins of the inn, including the recently acquired desk bell.

"Granny," Annie asked, concerned the game would trigger another episode, "how are you doing?"

"Peachy."

"Really?"

"Don't be silly." She looked up at Annie with clear, bright eyes. "Why wouldn't I be?"

"No reason." Annie breathed easier. Her grandmother was her usual self.

"We're just looking for my book. Thought it might be in here."

"What book?"

"You know, my book. The one I kept on a shelf in the sitting room."

Uh-oh. So much for being her usual self. Whatever book her grandmother had kept was surely lost.

"I don't think it's here, Granny," she said gently.

"Well, we'll have to go to the inn and find it."

"Maybe later." Annie had no intention of taking her grandmother there. It had been bad enough finding her at the inn ruins after one of her walkabouts. The place was far too dangerous for an old woman.

"Tomorrow?"

"We'll see."

The ringing of Annie's cell phone was the perfect excuse to end the conversation, until she glanced at the display and read the general store's number. She stepped out into the hall before answering the call.

"Hello, Gary. You on your way to pick up Nessa?" He was scheduled to take their daughter for a long weekend.

"Annie, hi. Actually, I'm still at work. My clerk for the evening shift is running late."

Gary frequently encountered staff problems. As the store's manager, it was his job to cover all shifts. Annie understood, but she was irritated nonetheless. Dempsey General Store and Trading Post had taken priority during the seven years of their marriage. It shouldn't take priority over their daughter.

"You're not coming?"

"I was hoping you could bring Nessa by the house. Linda Lee will meet you there."

Leave Nessa with his new wife? In their house, which, like the store, had escaped the fire? No way.

"What time will you be off work?"

"Not for several hours."

"You can pick her up then."

There was a long moment of silence before he replied. "Don't be difficult."

"Better yet, I'll drop her off at the store." Then Gary wouldn't have to see the apartment and remark, yet again, how small and cramped it was and how much extra room he and Linda Lee had.

"See you when you get here."

For whatever reason, he chose not to argue. Hurray for small favors.

"Nessa, honey, that was your dad."

Reentering the bedroom, Annie stopped in her tracks. While Nessa played with her favorite doll, Granny Orla sat on the bed cradling a pewter candlestick, tears streaming from her eyes.

Annie went over and kissed her grandmother's crinkly cheek. "Don't cry, Granny. We're going to be okay."

"I know that." She sniffed and patted Annie's arm. "It's just hard getting there."

After another kiss, Annie straightened and said, "Nessa, I'm going to drop you off at your dad's."

"When?"

"In a couple hours."

"After I go pony riding," she announced, moving her Barbie through the air as if it sat astride a galloping horse.

"What pony ride?"

"At the ranch. Where the cowboy lives. He promised."

Annie vaguely remembered Sam mentioning something last week when he dropped them off at the apartment. "Nessa, honey, he doesn't have a pony."

"He does. He told Grandma."

"Yes, the other night—"

"No, today."

"He called." Granny Orla sat up, showing signs of recovery. "After lunch. He talked to Fiona. Invited Nessa out for a pony ride."

Nessa jumped up from the bed and grabbed Annie's hand. "Can I go, Mommy? Please."

"Honey, you can't." She used her most coaxing tone. "I'm taking you to your dad's."

"Nooo!" Nessa dropped Annie's hand and threw herself onto the bed in typical three-year-old-not-getting-her-way fashion.

"Nessa, that's enough."

Annie's mother must have heard the noise. "What's all the fuss?" she asked from the doorway.

"Mom, did Sam invite Nessa over for a pony ride?"

"He mentioned the pony arrived today with a few other head from his ranch in California."

Nessa promptly launched herself off the bed and hugged Annie's waist. "Mommy, Mommy, I really wanna go."

"I wish you'd spoken with me first," Annie said to her mother.

"Nessa was there when Sam called. What was I supposed to do?" Fiona huffed, the most emotion she'd shown in a long time. "If you don't want to see Sam, just say so. I'll take Nessa and swing by her dad's after the pony ride."

"Yay!" Nessa danced in a circle. "Pony ride!"

"It's not that I don't want to see Sam," Annie protested.

Fiona's elevated eyebrows indicated differently.

Annie rubbed her throbbing temples. When had the world and everyone in it started conspiring against her? The insurance company. Gary. Her mother. Nessa. Sam.

She sighed. "One short pony ride. Now, where's your suitcase?"

If Nessa was going to the Golden Nugget, Annie would be the one taking her.

"Lovely. Have a good time," her mother said with rather suspicious-sounding satisfaction.

SAM DIDN'T EXPECT to see Annie's SUV driving in to the ranch, not after the way they'd parted the other night.

His day, which had gone poorly so far, significantly improved. More so when Granny Orla emerged from the passenger side, looking alert and cognizant of her surroundings. A huge improvement from the last time he'd seen her.

Fiona must have decided to stay home.

"Where's the pony?" Nessa skipped beside her mother, reminding Sam of Lyndsey when she was that age.

The happy days. At least, the happier days, when his and Trisha's marriage was working. Over the next few years, without really realizing it, they transformed into strangers who happened to cohabit.

"Welcome." He flashed Granny Orla, Nessa and Annie a big smile. Only Granny Orla and Nessa returned it. "The pony's in the barn. Come on."

"Mind if I have a look at the house?" Granny Orla didn't wait for a reply and started up the freshly raked gravel walkway.

"Not at all. Irma's in there. She's just finishing for the day."

"Wait!" Annie headed after Granny.

"I'll be fine." She shooed Annie away. "You and Nessa go on, have yourselves some fun."

Sam thought Nessa was probably going to have a lot more fun than her mother, judging by Annie's worried frown.

Conversation came to a complete halt on the way to the barn. Sam refused to be deterred and asked Annie, "How's work? Done with the erosion tests?"

"We'll be conducting different ones for weeks. Months, probably. Assessing the degree of burn and the land's ability to recover."

"Why isn't the pony with the other horses?" Nessa was evidently disinterested in any talk about her mother's work.

"She's too little to be in the corral. The other horses will bully her and steal all her food."

Lyndsey scrambled to her feet the moment they entered the barn. Except to eat and sleep, she kept a constant vigil on the kits. Annie had been right about her abandoning the idea of sleeping in the barn. One night on the hard floor and the kits' constant ruckus had been enough. Sam was not-so-secretly overjoyed.

"Hi." Lyndsey greeted Annie enthusiastically. "Are you here to see the kits?"

"I am," she answered as if that had been her plan all along. "Lyndsey, you remember Nessa."

Not at all shy, Nessa skipped over to the cage and knelt down beside it, her eyes enormous. "Mommy, look! Baby raccoons."

Delighted at having an audience other than her father, Lyndsey launched into a detailed report of the kits' progress during the last week. The baby raccoons obliged by acting adorable. Standing on their hind legs and vocalizing, they reached their small handlike paws through the cage wire.

"They don't need much kitten formula anymore," Lyndsey said. "They're mostly eating solid food."

She sounded a lot like Dr. Murry, who'd dropped by recently to examine the kits and pronounce them "thriving."

"I'm gonna ride a pony," Nessa said, the kits failing to keep her interest long.

Lyndsey rose after making sure the cage latch was secure. "I'll go with you."

And here Sam thought he'd have to coax his normally antisocial daughter.

He and Annie exchanged looks, their most intimate communication since his return to Sweetheart. To his relief, her frown was replaced with a smile.

It unbalanced him. For a second, she was the young woman from nine years ago. The one he'd loved—and left.

Must be the barn. They'd escaped here often. The loft, with its stacks of sweet-smelling hay, was one of their favorite places. Sam had liked picking pieces of hay out of Annie's hair and remembering how they'd gotten there. He never quite found them all and someone inevitably noticed.

Lyndsey took Nessa's hand and led her to the stalls.

"She's big!" Nessa came to an abrupt halt and stared dumbfounded at a half-draft mare who'd stuck her head out to investigate.

Sam chuckled. "That's not the pony."

Annie approached the mare, her hand extended. "Is she sick?"

Leave it to her to notice.

"The pony and another horse I had shipped here managed the trip just fine. This old girl, however, began showing signs of distress and refused to eat or drink. Will and I treated her for colic, just to be on the safe side."

"Did it help?" She brushed the mare's forelock as she studied her.

"At first she didn't respond. I was just getting ready to call Dr. Murry again when she suddenly began eating. I guess the ten-hour trailer ride must have upset her system."

"She still seems listless."

"I'm going to keep a close watch on her for the next day or two."

"What's the pony's name?" Nessa gripped the side of the stall door and perched on her tiptoes in an effort to see the equally short equine on the other side.

"Mooney." Lyndsey squeezed in beside her.

"Mooney? That's a silly name."

"It's a good name. She had a twin sister called Sunny."

"What's a twin?"

"That's when the mommy has two babies inside her tummy."

Nessa's small mouth fell open. "How do babies get inside the mommy's tummy?"

Annie stepped over to the girls, hastily running interference. "We'll talk about it later, sweetie, okay?"

"Okay." Nessa jumped up and down, her sneakers kicking the stall door. "I wanna ride the pony."

"Nessa, no. You'll break the door."

Without thinking, Sam lifted Nessa up by the waist so she could see into the stall. She let out a small, excited gasp.

"You don't have to—"

Sam cut off Annie's objection. "It's all right. I've got her."

She gave him another of those intimate looks. This one hit him square in the chest.

The pony, a pint-size dapple gray, came over to sniff the hand Nessa held out.

"Be careful she doesn't nip you. Pet her nose like this." Bracing Nessa with one arm, he showed her the correct way.

Nessa copied him and then squealed with delight when Mooney nuzzled her fingers.

"She likes me."

"What say we saddle her up so you can have a ride?"

Nessa's answer was to squirm excitedly until he set her on the ground.

"Have you ever ridden a horse before?" It was Lyndsey who posed the question, assuming the attitude of a more experienced rider.

Nessa shook her head, her expression solemn.

Sam got a kick out of the exchange.

"Actually, sweetie, you have ridden before. Sort of." Annie turned her attention to Sam. "Some friends of her dad have horses. We'd go riding with them once in a while. When we'd get back, Gary would put Nessa in the saddle with him and walk around a bit. I have some pictures—" She hesitated and drew a fortifying breath. "Had some pictures."

The loss of something precious and irreplaceable shone in her eyes. She must suffer that same emotion a dozen times a day.

"We'll take more pictures today." Sam held up his cell phone.

"Good idea."

Again, she aimed her glance directly at him. Again, the jolt hit him square in the chest.

They may not be ready for a relationship or ever be able to have one, given their rocky history, but that didn't stop Sam from devising reasons for inviting Annie to the ranch again.

Mooney hadn't been ridden much since Lyndsey decided she wanted a "real horse," but the pony remembered the drill perfectly. When Sam handed Nessa the lead rope, Mooney walked calmly beside her and stood patiently while Sam saddled and bridled her.

Lyndsey explained the entire process, instructing Nessa on how to sit in the saddle and hold the reins. All Nessa wanted to do was pet the pony.

Sam checked the girth and gave it one last tug, making sure the saddle wouldn't slip. "This used to belong to Lyndsey, until she grew too big. It's just right for you."

He made a mental note to purchase a few more child and youth saddles for the ranch's guests. Maybe another pony or two. While most of the horses were trustworthy enough to carry young riders, the children might feel safer on a smaller mount.

Lyndsey held the lead rope while Sam lifted Nessa onto Mooney's back. "I can take her," Lyndsey said.

"Are you sure?" Annie's anxious gaze darted from the pony to Lyndsey to Sam.

"Mooney's completely broke," he answered, placing the reins in Nessa's hands and adjusting her feet in the stirrups. "And Lyndsey's good with horses. Besides, Mooney's short and close to the ground. Nessa won't have far to fall."

"Sam!"

He grinned. Annie had always been gullible, and he'd enjoyed teasing her, refusing to stop until she gave him a kiss. And once they started kissing…

Sam reminded himself to stay focused on the girls.

Lyndsey took the lead, walking ahead of Nessa and the pony. Outside, the late-afternoon sun streamed through the pine trees, and Sam had them stop so he could snap several photos.

"Let's get one with you and Nessa."

Annie posed with her daughter, delight on both their faces, Annie's arm circling Nessa's waist. Sam thought he might keep a copy of this particular picture for himself.

"Thanks," she said when they were done, her tone warm with appreciation.

"I'll need your phone number or email address."

She recited the information without hesitation. A big difference from before.

Pleased with himself, Sam keyed the number and address into his phone contacts. If he kept this up, he'd eventually penetrate that invisible shield of armor she wore, one chink at a time.

"LYNDSEY'S REALLY PATIENT with Nessa," Annie observed.

Nessa had been riding the pony for about ten minutes, Annie and Sam walking behind the girls. Annie had been trying hard to avoid slipping into their former comfortable camaraderie.

Not easy. Memories had assailed her from the second she drove onto the Gold Nugget, even more than her visit last week. He was getting to her, and she'd have to be careful or risk a new heartache when he left.

"She's kind of bossy, if you ask me." Sam pushed back his cowboy hat then pulled it down again, a gesture she'd always found endearing. "To be honest, she doesn't have much experience with little kids. Her friends are mostly her own age." Deep furrows creased his brow. "I should've thought more about her missing her friends when I brought her here. Maybe that's why she's become so attached to the raccoons."

"You really think so?"

"Naw." He had to chuckle. "She's an animal lover. Like you."

"More like her dad, I'd say." Annie smiled and thought, *There, that wasn't so hard.*

"Dogs and horses are my kind of pets," he said. "Not wild animals."

"You were pretty tolerant of the ones I dragged home. Remember that magpie with the broken wing? You taught it to whistle 'Mary Had a Little Lamb.'"

"Then the darn thing wouldn't shut up."

"I was never so glad to release an animal back into the wild."

"Is that why you moped for three straight days?" He flashed her a grin, the heart-stopping kind.

Good grief, she should have known better than to bring up old times.

"You miss the animals?" he asked.

"I did. Do. Gary was never fond of animals, and my house was too small for pets anyway. When we divorced, and I moved back to the inn, I limited myself to the occasional stray dog and cat."

"Did you lose any pets in the fire?"

"Not in the fire. But our landlord doesn't allow animals. We had to find temporary homes for ours with friends in Reno."

"That must have been hard."

"Yeah." The sympathy in Sam's voice touched her. "Nessa really loves dogs."

"You two can visit the kits and pony anytime."

His hint to come back was as subtle as a sandbag dropped from a second-story window. Annie didn't mind as much as she should.

"We'd better head back." She glanced over her shoulder at the ranch house. They'd been walking the footpath that circled it and the barn, a remnant from the days of *The Forty-Niners.* According to the curator, Mrs. Litey, the film crew had created the path over years of filming scenes from different angles. "I have to drop Nessa off at her dad's in about an hour."

"You have time."

Annie did. She was using her ex as an excuse. Sam's charms were far too potent.

"Can I ask why you married him?"

She resisted answering the point-blank question. Too many unresolved feelings. She settled on "The usual reasons."

"Do you want my opinion?"

"Do I have a choice?" Thank goodness the girls were out of earshot.

"I think you weren't over me and he was handy."

Annie burst out laughing. "That's some ego you have."

"Seemed kind of quick to me. We'd hardly broken up when you and he started dating."

Her laughter died. "You were gone a year. Breaking up was a technicality."

"I was gone eleven months."

"Same difference. And, really, who are you to accuse me of jumping the gun? You married Trisha four months later, as I recall, and she was pregnant."

"I won't disagree, I probably should have waited. But I was miserable and susceptible after losing you. I called you every week during those eleven months."

"You started out calling me every week," she corrected him. "It didn't last."

"I came back for you. Like I promised I would."

"Only to tell me it was over!" She stopped and took a restoring breath. This wasn't the time to lose her temper.

"Not how I remember it."

"You think *I* ended things?"

"That's what happened."

Un-freaking-believable. "No, it's not. You said we were through."

"Because you said you were tired of waiting. That read *breakup* to me."

"I thought…hoped…you were coming back for good. And you didn't. Wouldn't." She bit her lower lip. All these years it still hurt. "Which you made crystal clear."

"You were angry at me for taking the job in California."

Anger had hardly begun to describe her emotions. She'd wanted to marry Sam. For the two of them to have the kind of life she'd always dreamed of. Cozy cabin, white picket fence, two beautiful children. She was determined to be the first Hennessy woman in three generations to hold on to her man.

Then Sam appeared at her door one evening, telling her he'd found a job at a cattle ranch north of Sacramento. One that paid better and offered more opportunity.

She should have realized he wasn't ready for marriage, that she'd been pushing him too hard. Their young ages weren't the only reason for his reluctance. And it wasn't true that Sam hadn't loved her.

He'd needed to establish himself before he settled down. Make his mark on the world, like his father and brother in Ohio. But Annie had been impatient, and look what that got her.

"I wanted you to come with me."

His words tugged at her heart. "I couldn't leave. This is my home, the inn was my family's business."

"You could have left for a year. Hell, for a visit even. I needed experience, enough to land a foreman's job."

"Which you got when you married Trisha."

He shook his head. "My father-in-law cut no one slack, including me. I wasn't promoted for four years. Not until I'd earned it. And I'll thank him for that always. He's a great man and a good judge of character. He saw potential in me I didn't know I had."

She was wrong. Sam hadn't been handed the job as a wedding gift.

"I'm glad for you."

"But you're still hurt I started seeing Trisha right away."

"Okay. You win. I'm hurt and carrying a grudge. Can we not argue anymore? What's the point?"

For several moments, humming insects and their footsteps on the dirt path were the only sounds.

Sam spoke first. "There are a lot of things in my life I'd change if I could, including that."

"I really am sorry Trisha died." Annie's residual pain over their breakup was nothing compared to losing a spouse.

"Me, too." His gaze followed the girls' progress as they disappeared behind the barn.

Annie might be more concerned about Nessa if Lyndsey weren't such a competent riding instructor and the pony as docile as she was cute.

"It was never my intention to hurt you. Or Trisha," he added softly.

His sincerity didn't ease the lingering sorrow inside her. "What was it Granny used to say? Marry in haste, repent at leisure." Annie was silent a moment. "Guess I should have listened myself."

"Was your marriage to Gary that bad?"

"Not at first."

"What went wrong, if I can ask?"

She hadn't loved him. How could she when she'd been still in love with Sam? "We grew apart."

"Easy to do when you're not close to start with."

"We were close. Initially."

"I wasn't talking about you and Gary."

Sam and his wife had had problems? Despite his marriage being the result of an unplanned pregnancy, Annie had assumed he and Trisha were content, if not blissful.

"We made a go of it," he said. "For a while. Because of Lyndsey. I'm not sure exactly when we stopped trying."

"Gary and I stopped trying after the first year."

"Why did you stay married?"

"You really have to ask?" She gave a derisive snort. "I'm a Hennessy."

"It's just stupid gossip, Annie. Busybodies with too much time on their hands. Your family isn't cursed."

She smiled ruefully. "Funny thing is, dating Gary immediately after you left didn't lessen the gossip. If anything, we gave people more to talk about when our marriage started circling the drain. Gary was on the verge of leaving me when I got pregnant. I convinced him a child would change everything. It didn't."

Sam reached for her, his strong fingers curving around her neck and sliding into her hair. "We're quite the pair."

The sparks were instantaneous, like always with the two of them. They'd fight, then they'd make up. Lots of making up.

Annie steeled herself. She could not, would not, kiss him. In fact, she was marching ahead right this second and finding the girls. Except her feet didn't move.

Her body did. It leaned into him, the tug a familiar one. She could no more resist Sam today than she could years ago. He had only to look at her and she was in his arms, lifting her mouth to meet his hot, urgent kiss.

When, she dimly wondered, had she lost control? When had she ever really exercised it?

Annie might have pondered the questions longer if she wasn't entirely taken over by Sam and the electric sensation of his lips on hers. Sliding over them. Coaxing them apart. Making way for his tongue to enter and taste her completely.

Oh, heavens! This was insane. She'd let revisiting their painful past erode her defenses. And now look. She and Sam were kissing.

He expertly applied the right amount of pressure with his mouth as his arms circled her waist and fitted her snug against him. Hard to soft. Taking and giving. Demanding and yielding.

Annie was forced to stand on her tiptoes or break off the kiss. To ensure that didn't happen, she anchored herself to him by gripping his shoulders. Then she released the tight hold on her emotions and let herself feel.

Only Sam. Only them. Only this moment.

This was how he used to kiss her, and kept kissing her until she didn't know where she was.

Where she was. The girls!

Annie pushed abruptly away from him, a groan escaping. She'd let Sam kiss her. She'd kissed him back. And their daughters were…

"Nessa! Lyndsey! Come back!" She frantically scanned the immediate area.

"They're just around the corner," Sam said.

Thank God. She shuddered to think of the explaining required if the girls had caught them.

"We shouldn't have done that," she stammered.

"Speak for yourself."

"Sam. We can't… I won't…"

He laughed. Laughed! "Still the same old Annie."

Before she could utter her first word of protest, the girls charged out from behind the barn, Lyndsey running and the pony, Nessa on its back, trotting beside her.

"Dad, Dad," Lyndsey hollered. "Look what we found." She carried something in her arms, grappling with it and the reins.

Annie used the three spare seconds afforded her to smooth her hair and straighten her shirt.

Sam, naturally, didn't have a single hair or piece of clothing out of place. With unflappable nonchalance, he asked, "What is it?"

"A cat." She held out a scrawny feline, which meowed plaintively. "It was hiding in a bush. Can we keep him? I'm calling him Sylvester."

Annie couldn't ever remember being so glad to see a cat in her life. Had it not distracted the girls…

What had she been thinking?

And that was the problem in a nutshell. When it came to Sam, all thinking, along with good judgment and common sense, went by the wayside.

Chapter Six

Annie shouldered open the door to the Dempsey General Store and Trading Post. Gary had worked here as a clerk when they started dating. During their marriage, he was promoted twice, taking over as manager when his predecessor retired two years ago last spring.

His new wife worked alongside him. Assistant manager or head salesclerk or whatever. She always wore the clothing the store sold: T-shirts with scenes of Sweetheart and quaint sayings about getting married, ball caps with deer or Conestoga wagons or linked gold rings on the front, thin rope necklaces holding a flask of liquid in which flecks of fool's gold floated, frilly blue garters. She liked to wear those on her arms.

Annie didn't know how long Gary and his wife would have to be married before she dropped the *new* and called Linda Lee by her name. Probably when Annie and the town stopped thinking of her as "Gary's ex."

Personally, she thought Linda Lee went overboard in her dress and attitude. The customers, however, seemed to appreciate—if not adore—her. At least, they used to. There weren't many customers in the store these days, adoring or otherwise.

"Daddy, Daddy!" Nessa charged ahead of Annie and Granny Orla. The little girl loved the store, especially the toy section.

Truthfully, Annie had loved the store, too—long before

Gary went to work there. Some might say the shelves were loaded with cheap, touristy junk. After all, who really needed a fake bear hide or plastic talking fish? But the general store's log exterior and rustic decor had a charm that she found appealing.

As a child, her mother would let her ride her bike there to pick up some small necessity for the kitchen or one of the inn's guests. Even after Annie was old enough to drive, she still preferred to ride her bike.

That was how she and Sam had met. On the hill near Cohea Ridge where he and another wrangler were moving cows across the forest service road from one section of grazing range to another. She was training for a charity cycling event.

Her first glimpse of him was herding a recalcitrant calf through the gate. She'd stopped, watching till he was done, already falling for him.

He'd trotted over, tall and handsome in the saddle, and asked her out on the spot.

"Daddy, where are you?" Nessa called.

Annie blinked herself back to the present.

"Right here," Gary answered.

Nessa dashed down an aisle bulging with calendars, books, magazines and postcards, following the sound of her father's voice.

"I'm going to see if there are any of those chocolate mint cookies I like." Granny Orla also disappeared to scour the food section.

That left Annie on her own, not a place she wanted to be at this moment. Without any company, she had nothing to distract her from thoughts of Sam, the past and the kiss they'd just shared.

The kiss they'd just shared.

Such a mundane assessment describing an occurrence that had turned her already upside-down world on its side. Much like their first kiss soon after that meeting on Cohea Ridge eleven years ago.

He'd taken her to the ice cream parlor. She remembered thinking afterward that he'd tasted yummy. Like the hot fudge sundae she'd eaten.

He'd tasted yummy today, too, and his effect on her was no different.

She really was an idiot, learning nothing from the past.

It wouldn't happen again, of that she was certain. Sam Wyler wouldn't get to her, and she'd start by putting him far from her mind.

Holding on to Nessa's weekend bag, she strolled the same aisle her daughter had taken, only at a much slower pace. In the back of the store, Gary and his *new* wife were unpacking a shipment of mining equipment. Why bother? Amateur rock hounds and gold seekers were as scarce as honeymooners, what with most of the popular areas having been ravaged by the fire.

Annie hesitated, observing from behind a display. Gary and Linda Lee were comfortable with each other, like an old married couple rather than a new one. The smiles they exchanged were sweet and intimate.

Had she and Gary ever been like that? A little perhaps. Once.

She and Sam had been like that. Right up to the evening he told her about the job in California.

"Hey, there!" Gary's new wife straightened from the open box on the floor and smiled brightly, greeting Annie as if they were on the best of terms.

Linda Lee. She really had to start calling her that. "Sorry I'm late."

"No worries. We've been hearing all about the pony ride. How exciting!"

"That was nice of Sam," Gary said.

It sounded strange, hearing him speak Sam's name. The

two men had known each other casually back when Sam lived here, but they hadn't been friends. Later, Gary had hated being compared to Sam. Not by Annie. It was the gossips who couldn't keep quiet.

"He had some horses from the ranch in California shipped here," Annie explained. "One of them was a pony."

"And he bought the entire string from High Country Out-fitters," Linda Lee added.

"News travels fast."

"Oh, no! He told us. When he was in here yesterday."

Sam had visited the general store and spent time talking to Gary and Linda Lee?

That shouldn't bother Annie, yet for some reason it did. Had they discussed her? She wouldn't put it past either man. They were probably curious about each other and her relationships with them. Past and present.

"We found a stray cat." Nessa's announcement was perfectly timed. "It's black-and-white and really skinny. Lyndsey named him Sylvester."

"Are you keeping it?" Gary's tone carried a hint of alarm. He only just tolerated cats.

"Can we, Mommy?" Nessa asked.

"No, honey. We aren't allowed to have any pets in the apartment."

Another reminder of their circumstances and the four-legged family members they'd had to find temporary homes for.

"I suppose we could take the cat," Gary said.

Linda Lee jumped on the bandwagon. "What a great idea. Then it would be yours whenever you stay with us."

"I'm gonna have a cat." Nessa bounced up and down with excitement.

Annie wanted to scream. This was so unfair. She was the cat lover, not Gary. He'd only agreed in order to look like the world's greatest dad in front of Nessa and Linda Lee.

"The cat belongs to Lyndsey," Annie said, proud of the control she exercised. "She's the one who found it."

"She might give it to us if we ask," Linda Lee suggested. "Sam mentioned they were returning to California in about a month."

Sam again? Annie's control wavered.

She shouldn't care. *Didn't* care. Sam was not some possession of hers. While he was in Sweetheart he was going to interact with people. People including her ex-husband. And there was nothing she could do about it.

"Nessa," Annie began, "let's see what happens first."

"But I want a cat." She pouted. "And a pony."

Annie waited for either Gary or Linda Lee to promise a pony, too. "If you found a cat," she said, "you wouldn't want someone to take it from you."

"Your mother's right." Gary tweaked Nessa's ear.

Annie bit back her surprise. Before his marriage, he'd been supportive of her. Shortly after, he started siding with Nessa, often forcing Annie to be the tough mom. She hated it.

"We'll get you another cat," he said. "The pet warehouse store in Lake Tahoe is always sponsoring adoption events."

"Of course we will," Linda Lee confirmed.

"Yay!" Nessa threw her arms around her father's legs.

The scream Annie had suppressed earlier echoed inside her head. Having Gary undermine her in front of their daughter was bad enough. Now she had Linda Lee doing it, too.

"Annie." Granny Orla appeared, her arms laden with boxes of mint cookies and an assortment of other snacks. "There you are. I'm ready whenever you are. Oh, hi, Gary. And…" She scrutinized Linda Lee. "I'm sorry, dear, but your name has slipped my mind."

"Linda Lee."

"That's right." She turned and winked at Annie. "Don't know why I keep forgetting."

Though it was wrong on many levels, Annie took pleasure in her grandmother's faked memory loss.

"Annie, I forgot my purse." Granny Orla held out her purchases.

"I'll pay."

"On the house," Gary said, giving Granny Orla a friendly smile.

"Why, thank you!"

Something about the mischievous glint in her grandmother's eyes made Annie think this had been the plan all along. She felt even better.

"We should get going." She set the weekend bag by Gary's feet and gave Nessa a hug and kiss. "You be a good girl. I love you." This was the hardest part of her and Gary's shared custody agreement.

"I'll walk you out," he said when Annie straightened.

"That's not necessary."

"Be right back," he told Nessa and Linda Lee.

"No worries." Linda Lee unearthed a large round prospecting pan from the shipping box and handed it to Nessa, an isn't-she-darling expression on her face. "I've got my little helper with me."

Annie tried not to think of Linda Lee as Nessa's stepmom. Or Nessa's fascination with the prospecting pan and whatever else the box contained.

"What is it, Gary?" Annie asked when they were outside.

"Hold on a second." He opened the SUV's passenger side door for Granny Orla.

"I don't want to leave her sitting there," Annie warned.

"She'll be fine."

Granny Orla was already opening a box of cookies.

"I can't stay long," Annie reminded him. "I have to get up at five."

"It's Nessa."

She should have seen this coming. Gary didn't steal private moments with her except to talk about Nessa or their divorce or Annie's plans for the future.

"She doesn't need a cat. We have two, which we'll get back as soon as we rebuild the inn."

The lines bracketing Gary's mouth deepened. "I'd like you to consider letting her stay with me and Linda Lee more often."

"No." Annie was amazed at her outward calm. Inside, a maelstrom raged. "You are not getting full custody."

"I'm not asking for full custody. Just more frequent custody. Until you're back on your feet."

"Which will be soon. We're on the verge of settling with the insurance company."

"My point exactly. You've got a lot on your plate at the moment. Working. The inn. Nessa. I can make things easier for you."

"Taking Nessa away from me isn't making things easier."

"I'm trying to help."

Annie was hearing that a lot lately. First Sam, now Gary. Granted, she had taken a hard knock, but she was more than capable of pulling herself back up.

"I know you love Nessa—" she began.

"And I only want what's best for her."

Annie tried not to take his remark as an implication that she couldn't provide adequately for their daughter. Still, it felt that way.

"You'd have more room in the apartment," he said. "And she'd have more room at my house. Just think about it."

"I get that you hate the apartment. But Nessa's perfectly happy there."

"Her happiness isn't what's worrying me. It's her safety." He took hold of Annie's arm and drew her away from the SUV and Granny Orla's curious stare. "Let's be honest, your grandmother's becoming very forgetful. And your mother…"

"What about my mother?"

"We both know she's struggling. Emotionally."

Though everything Gary said was true, Annie's defenses soared. "Yes, she has moments when she's down. Who wouldn't in her shoes? But you're not the only one with concerns. I have my own about you."

"Me?"

"What's with the new prospecting equipment? Business in the store is practically at a standstill. Who's to say how long you and Linda Lee will have jobs?"

"It's going to pick up. As soon as Sam's guest ranch opens."

Had Gary just brought up Sam a third time?

"He isn't a miracle worker. It's going to take more than converting the Gold Nugget into a guest ranch to revitalize this town. It's going to take the Sweetheart Inn." Her voice gained conviction. "This is a place where couples come to get married and honeymoon."

"They can do that at the Gold Nugget, too."

Annie switched tactics. "Letting Nessa run around the store while you and Linda Lee are waiting on customers isn't any better day care than my mother can provide."

"We're considering putting her in preschool."

"Preschool?" Annie was aghast. "You decided this without consulting me?"

"I was going to talk to you."

This went beyond anything Gary had done. Just how much influence did his *new* wife have on him?

Fear gave way to terror. "You can't take her. I'll fight you."

"Relax. I'm not taking Nessa from you. This is just preschool we're talking about."

And more frequent custody. If Annie thought she could get away with it, she'd rush back inside the store and grab their daughter. Gary would stop her, however, and the last thing Annie wanted was to make a scene in front of Nessa and Linda Lee.

"I'll be by the usual time to pick up Nessa," she said briskly.

"We're not done talking about this."

"I agree."

"And I'm going to adopt a cat."

"Do whatever you feel you have to." Turning away, she climbed into the SUV and rolled down the window. "Just because Linda Lee hasn't gotten pregnant yet is no reason for her to take my child."

His features hardened. "That's not the reason."

Annie had crossed a line. Which wouldn't help her cause. Gary was relentless when riled.

She and her grandmother left without saying goodbye. At the end of the street, she pulled over, the tremors racking her body too severe for her to continue driving.

"That man is heartless," Granny Orla said, and then called him a name Annie couldn't recall ever having passed her grandmother's lips.

The shock of hearing it eased her tremors.

It didn't eliminate her fear.

"He's just jerking your chain," Granny Orla said. "He's not serious."

Annie would give anything—*everything*—for that to be true.

THE PAIR OF YOUNG Nubian goats was harder to catch than any fleet-footed calf. Sam took a break, wiping a palm across his sweaty brow. Maybe he should try roping them.

"Thanks." He scowled at Will, who leaned against his truck hood, watching Sam make an idiot of himself. "This is your fault."

The man just shrugged.

"You could help me at least."

"Could. But this is more fun."

"For you."

Will, who seldom showed much emotion, grinned.

He'd delivered the goats thirty minutes ago after calling Sam. A family Will knew was moving, having lost their place in the fire, and wanted to find good homes for their various livestock. Sam thought the goats might come in handy during the gymkhanas and amateur rodeos he was planning for his guests. Plus, the youngsters were bound to enjoy them.

It didn't occur to him when he gave Will the okay that the demon goats would leap from the horse trailer and taunt Sam with the chase of his life.

They abruptly stopped circling the yard to munch on a rosebush. Sam crept up on them, only to have them dart off at the last second. Running in hot pursuit, he lost his footing and nearly fell before righting himself. That earned him a chuckle from Will.

"If you're not careful, I'm going to fire you." Sam braced his hands on his knees, his breathing labored.

"I got a lead on a man selling his roping equipment. He supposedly needs the cash and is ready to talk."

Roping equipment? Another guest-related purchase Sam was considering. "What kind of equipment?"

"A Heel-O-Matic, training dummies, chutes."

Other than lariats, it was everything he'd need. "Fine, you're not fired."

"Didn't think so." Will started off toward the corrals.

"Wait!"

Will kept going.

Just as Sam was cussing the man, Lyndsey emerged from the barn, evidently taking a break from baby-raccoon sitting. Sylvester, the new barn cat, padded after her. He preferred outside to inside and disdained everyone other than Lyndsey.

Sam had insisted they post Cat Found signs around town. As of yet, no one had claimed Sylvester. Singed fur on his back and a starved appearance suggested he had run off during the fire and taken up the life of a stray. Perhaps his owners had already relocated from Sweetheart.

Lyndsey's face lit up at the sight of the Nubians, and she hurried toward them. The pair had stopped to make a snack of the blackberry bushes growing alongside the house.

"Where did the goats come from?"

Rather than run away, they merely lifted their heads and bleated. As if to further humiliate Sam, they stood perfectly still while she knelt beside them and hugged their thin necks.

He muttered under his breath.

"They're so cute. Look at these ears." She stroked the closest one, whose long ears, like its mate's, hung down to frame its funny, yet charming, face. "Are we keeping them?"

Sam came over, and while the goats did cast him the evil eye, they didn't run off. "We are."

Even if he hadn't already agreed to take them, he doubted he could pry the goats loose from his daughter. Her collection of displaced animals just grew by two new members.

Annie had been the same way, instantly connecting with every creature she encountered, wild or tame.

They hadn't seen each other since the evening of the pony ride and their kiss. Two days. Sam had resisted driving by her apartment on his visit to town that morning. She wouldn't appreciate seeing him anyway, if the way she'd hastily gathered Nessa and departed was any indication.

Kissing her might have been a mistake, but he was very glad he'd done it. At the first sensation of her mouth on his, long-buried feelings shot to the surface. He hadn't been able to shake them since. Nor did he want to.

"Where are we going to keep them?" Lyndsey stood. The moment she took a step forward, the goats followed her like besotted puppy dogs. Figured.

"I think in the empty stall."

The pony had taken up permanent residence in one of the barn's three box stalls. Another was occupied by the half-draft mare from California. Her listlessness and loss of appetite had returned. Then, starting yesterday, she'd begun coughing, and discharge leaked from her nostrils.

Sam had placed a call to Dr. Murry, Sweetheart's only vet, and received a message the man was out of town. He'd yet to decide his next course of action.

"I'll take them." Lyndsey started pulling on the ropes tied around the goats' necks. "What do they eat?"

"We can give them hay and pellets for now. I'll pick up some goat chow on my next trip to the feed store."

The sound of tires crunching on gravel didn't rouse Sam's interest. With the arrival of the construction crew, vehicles of all kinds were constantly coming and going, even on this warm Sunday afternoon.

Then he noticed the town's logo painted on the side of the sedan and went to greet his newest visitor. Though it had been years, he recognized the woman right away.

"Mayor Dempsey. Good to see you." To Sam's surprise, the passenger side door opened, and Granny Orla stepped out. "Granny, what are you doing here?"

"She was walking down the road," Mayor Dempsey said, pumping Sam's hand enthusiastically. "Said she was coming here. Seeing as I was already heading in this direction, I gave her a lift. And called Annie," she continued in a whisper. "Sometimes Granny gets disoriented."

"I know. I gave her a ride home myself last week."

Granny Orla didn't bother saying hello to Sam. She just went directly toward the house.

"Irma's not working today," he hollered after her.

She didn't turn around.

"Should we go after her?" Mayor Dempsey wore a worried frown.

"She'll be all right. I think she likes to wander the place. Brings back memories for her."

"Her affair with the show's star was quite the scandal in

the day. Some folks wondered if Fiona wasn't his daughter. Of course, she's not." The mayor gestured dismissively. "Fiona was three or four when *The Forty-Niners* started production. I know because we were in Sunday school together."

Sam tried to imagine Granny Orla as a young, attractive woman. It wasn't hard. She'd probably been quite the looker and, single mother or not, able to catch the eye of a handsome TV actor.

"How long ago did the ranch close to the public?" Sam asked.

"Been three years now. It changed hands several times before then. When old Mrs. Litey retired, that was pretty much the end. The new owners weren't interested in replacing her."

"Whatever happened to her?" Sam's memories of the ranch's curator were fond ones.

"She still lives in town. In a seniors' group home that, luckily, wasn't destroyed by the fire."

"I'd like to visit her."

"You can, but I doubt she'll remember you. She has advanced Alzheimer's."

It was the second-worst news Sam had received since returning to Sweetheart, the first being that Annie's inn had burned down. "That's a shame."

"Indeed." The mayor's glance traveled to the construction vehicles and small army of workers. "My, my, this has become one busy place."

"We're just starting."

"I've been wanting to stop by and tell you how happy we are you're remodeling the ranch. And grateful. You're doing a lot for our little town. Cora Abrams and the Fiersteins have both mentioned using your construction contractor for their renovations. I don't know how or why you're picking up the contractor's profit."

Sam was glad the head baker at the local caterers and the owners of the ice cream shop would be staying. "It's not as much as you think. Chas agreed to lower his profit in exchange for all the business. The slow economy's been hard on construction companies."

"With your help, Sweetheart will be back on its feet before long."

He ignored the remorse eating away at him. He couldn't have single-handedly spared the town, but he should have tried harder. "The ranch is a good investment."

"Well, you could have chosen elsewhere. We're glad you didn't. And glad you came back. You're one of our own, Sam."

"I've often thought about coming back."

Mayor Dempsey checked her watch. "I hate to run, but I'm needed at the bar." Besides heading local government, Hilda Dempsey owned and operated the Paydirt Saloon, an iconic bar and grill that was originally built by the first Dempseys to settle in Sweetheart back in the 1850s.

"Thanks for bringing Granny Orla by," Sam said.

"I didn't want her wandering the roads alone."

Small towns might have their disadvantages. Looking after their own wasn't one of them. Granny Orla would always have someone willing to pick her up and take her home.

Sam and Lyndsey had barely gotten the two goats, Yogi and Boo Boo—clearly he let his daughter watch too many cartoons—into the stall when Annie arrived.

He walked out of the barn at the same moment she slammed the door of her SUV. His breath caught. This was the first time he'd seen her out of uniform. Denim capris showed off her slim legs and curvy hips. A tiny T-shirt hugged her trim waist. Her shiny brunette hair, normally contained by clips or bands for work, hung in bouncy waves around her face.

"Hi." He met up with her halfway to the house. "Your grandmother's inside."

God give him strength. She wore some kind of shiny pink lip gloss. Cherry? Strawberry? A desire to taste it all but consumed him.

"Sorry about this," she said.

"No problem."

He didn't expect her to mention their kiss the other night. Neither would he bring it up and risk scaring her off any sooner than necessary. But it sure was on his mind.

Rather than go inside as he expected, she paused at the front door. "I didn't realize how much work was going on here until I drove in."

"The crew's converting the bunkhouse into three separate guest bedrooms with a shared bathroom. They're scheduled to finish by the end of next week. Then we can start taking reservations."

"So soon?" She sounded impressed but not enthused.

"The architect suggested converting the bunkhouse. We'll use the kitchen in the main house to serve meals until the dining hall is completed. We're also constructing a second bunkhouse and three private cabins."

"Quite an undertaking."

"That's not all. We're enlarging the barn to include an office and clearing land for an arena."

"Arena?"

"A small one. In the meantime, we're using the back pasture. I'm thinking of having a larger cabin constructed for Lyndsey and me. That way, we can open the ranch house back up for tours. There are a lot of fans of the TV show out there."

She nodded silently. "I'll fetch my grandmother."

Sam could have kicked himself. Here Annie was desperately trying to rebuild her family's inn, and he was rambling on and on about the ranch. The one she had wanted to own one day.

"Annie." He reached for her arm.

She kept walking. "We can't stay."

He refused to let her go yet and went after her. "I have a favor to ask."

"Not a good time." Her tone was clipped as she opened the front door.

"I have a sick mare."

That brought her to a halt.

"Is there any chance you can look at her?"

Sam knew he was taking advantage of her soft side where animals were concerned. It didn't stop him. He'd utilize whatever tactics available to him to breach her defenses…

…and didn't let himself think about what he'd find on the other side if he succeeded.

Chapter Seven

"Who are these two?" Annie asked.

"Yogi Bear and Boo Boo." Sam shrugged at the names. "Our newest additions, thanks to Will."

"They're cute."

"And a lot of trouble."

"They like me!" Lyndsey glowed.

She was in the stall with the goats, dividing her time equally between them and the kits and leaving very little for Sam.

He missed her. Then again, she was happy caring for the animals. The happiest she'd been in a year and a half. He was either making the best or worst decision of his life.

"They don't like me," he grumped.

"Hmm." Annie gave him a lingering once-over. "What did you do to them?"

"Nothing."

Lyndsey rolled her eyes. "He chased them."

"They were eating the rosebushes and blackberries," Sam protested.

An amused and very appealing glint lit Annie's eyes. "That's reasonable."

Lyndsey came over to stand with Sam and Annie outside the mare's stall.

"Isn't she the draft horse from California?" Annie had offered only mild resistance when Sam had propelled her into the barn.

"Yeah. She was here when Nessa rode the pony." The same evening he and Annie had kissed.

She was remembering, too. Her quick, guilty glance in his direction gave her away.

"Is she doing any better?" She opened the stall door and stepped inside. The mare didn't so much as lift her head.

"I thought at first she hadn't traveled well. Then yesterday, she developed a cough and nasal discharge."

"You called Dr. Murry?"

"He's out of town until Tuesday. Fishing with his sons."

"I'm not sure how much help I can be."

"She's really sick. And seeing as you're here…"

More tugging on Annie's emotional heartstrings. Sam should be ashamed of himself.

"Poor girl," she crooned. "Feeling bad?" She ran her hand along the mare's chest and underneath her shoulder. "You're warm. You have a fever." Next, Annie lifted the mare's head to study her watery eyes and runny nose.

"Could be a simple respiratory virus. Or something much more serious, like equine herpes or strangles. You really need to have her looked at by a vet."

"I agree. But the next-closest large-animal clinic is in Lake Tahoe. They're not open on Sundays. I called." Sam leaned against the stall door. "If she's not better by tomorrow, I'll have Will trailer her there. In the meantime, I was hoping there was something you could do."

"Is she eating and drinking?"

He shook his head. "Not at all."

"You might try adding electrolytes to her water," Annie continued. "How much penicillin have you given her?"

"None yet."

"Sam!" She glared at him accusingly. "You know enough about horse care to give penicillin."

"I was heading to the feed store, then the mayor and Granny Orla arrived."

"The feed store doesn't carry equine medications. But Doc Murry keeps a supply at his house, along with Bute paste. That'll help with the fever. I'll call his wife."

"Come with me," Sam said.

"I really should get home."

"Please. I'm not good with needles." That was the truth, and she knew it.

"What about Will? He must have experience."

"I heard his truck pull out a few minutes ago."

"I can't leave my grandmother." Annie frowned.

Sam refused to be deterred. "We'll bring her along."

"I want to come, too," Lyndsey said.

He ruffled her hair. "Wouldn't think of leaving you behind."

"Yay!" The beaming smile she sent him arrowed straight into his heart.

He'd been waiting eighteen long months for that. "What say we stop on the way back for an ice cream cone? To go."

"The ice cream shop burned." Annie's words hung on the air.

How could he have forgotten so quickly? He'd driven by what was left of the shop just the other day, recalling how he'd taken Annie there for sundaes on their first date. Watching her lick chocolate syrup off her spoon, he'd become instantly smitten.

"The I Do Café serves ice cream." It was the only restaurant open for business, other than the Paydirt Saloon.

"Mom's fixing dinner," Annie said.

Sam made one last-ditch effort. "I promise to have you and Granny Orla home in plenty of time."

He thought for sure he'd blown his chance. Annie's brisk nod of agreement came as a surprise. "I'll go with you to Doc Murry's. Not the café, though."

"I want ice cream." Lyndsey tugged on his hand.

"We'll stop at the general store."

Another thoughtless suggestion. Annie's ex-husband managed the General Store and Trading Post.

"Later. After dinner," he amended. "First, we go to Dr. Murry's."

Sam and Annie found Granny Orla in the parlor. She was staring at the framed photographs on the walls, though she must have seen them a hundred times.

She smiled when they neared and pointed to one of the pictures. "I remember when this was taken."

"You were there?" Sam asked.

"I'm in the picture. So is Fiona. We were recruited as extras for the shoot."

Sam scrutinized the photo. Annie did, too.

"Well, lookie there." He smiled when he recognized two figures in the foreground outfitted in prairie clothes.

Annie's features were thoughtful. "You and Mom used to talk about being in the show."

"Those were the days." Granny sighed.

"Why did the producers ever choose Sweetheart for the location?" Sam asked.

"The ranch house. They were looking at historical areas, actual stops along the wagon train routes, to give the show authenticity. The house was already here, though in disrepair."

"Did Mayor Dempsey's family own it?"

"It was one of the few properties they didn't. The owners were actually distant cousins of ours. They all moved away decades ago and were more than happy to sell the place to the show. I can't count the number of times it's changed hands since then."

"I hope this is the last time."

"Me, too." Granny's fingers lightly traced the picture frame. "Lord, he was a handsome man." No doubt she was referring to the star of the show, who figured prominently in the photograph. "He asked me to go with him to Hollywood when the series ended."

"Why didn't you?" Sam asked.

"The inn. I couldn't leave it."

Did Annie realize her answer had been exactly the same when he implored her to go to California with him? It was also the reason why she hadn't attended veterinary school.

What was it about the Sweetheart Inn that chained the Hennessy women to it, even when it had been wiped off the face of the earth?

"We'd better go," Annie said.

Was she ever not in a hurry to leave?

After informing Chas, the contractor, of their plans, they piled into Sam's truck. During the drive, Annie placed a call to Dr. Murry's wife, who was home and agreed to sell them the needed medicine and syringes from her husband's supply.

This was hardly Sam's first trip to town since arriving in Sweetheart, yet it felt new as he viewed it through Annie's eyes.

Nothing looked the same, even the houses and buildings untouched by the fire. Those with scorched exteriors and sunken roofs saddened him. Vacant ground where a familiar structure had once stood left a gaping hole inside him.

Of the two wedding chapels in Sweetheart, one was gone. The other—Annie's favorite—had survived unscathed but stood empty, padlocks on the door.

There were signs of renewal. Several homes and businesses had begun the repair process, but their revamped appearances only added to the strangeness of the town.

Sam watched Annie as they drove by what remained of the inn. She stared quietly until they'd passed, then returned her attention to the road. The gaping hole inside him grew.

"Four summers volunteering with the Hotshots, and I still don't understand fires," he mused out loud. "Why they destroy one building and leave its neighbor intact. There's no rhyme or reason to it."

With the inn behind them, Annie had visibly relaxed. "I thought you only volunteered two summers."

Another inadvertent slipup. Sam ground his teeth together. To admit he'd led one of the crews battling the fire would require him to reveal his part in the town's demise.

"Well...I..."

"Daddy's a firefighter."

"Was a firefighter," Sam corrected Lyndsey, hoping she'd drop the subject.

No such luck.

"He was here. He told me all about it when he called."

"In Sweetheart?" She turned curious eyes on him.

"Not in town," he hedged. "Nearby."

"How near?"

They turned onto the dirt drive leading to the Murrys' house. Sam parked in front of the garage. No one made a move to get out.

"I joined the Redding California Hotshots last summer. I was having difficulties coping with Trisha's death. The hard physical labor, spending time away from the ranch, gave me a chance to work off my stress."

"I see."

"We were called to the fire on the third day."

"While it was still near Montgomery Canyon? Before it changed direction and headed to Sweetheart?"

He nodded. "We traveled with the fire as it moved across the canyon to Cohea Ridge."

"Why didn't you tell me?"

"I never found the right moment."

"You were there," she repeated, and sat back, appearing to absorb this information.

Sam wished he could read what was behind her guarded

expression. There'd been a time her thoughts and emotions weren't a secret to him.

"That must have been hard for you," Granny Orla said from the backseat. "Watching the town you cared about burn. Knowing the people in it. Knowing us."

Sam met her gaze in the rearview mirror. "You have no idea."

"Well, it's no wonder you avoid talking about it."

Annie said nothing, but Sam didn't think she agreed with her grandmother. She threw open her door and climbed out.

He left the truck running and the air conditioner on. "We won't be long," he told Lyndsey and Granny Orla, then headed toward the house.

Sam had the distinct impression he and Annie weren't done with this conversation.

Mrs. Murry was as affable as her husband. She'd assembled syringes, a bottle of penicillin and a tube of Bute in a brown paper bag for Sam and Annie. After thanking her profusely and promising to call her husband for an update on the mare, Sam returned to the truck with Annie.

Before they reached it, Sam stopped her. "I'm sorry. I should have told you about my crew fighting the fire. You have every right to be angry with me."

"I'm not angry with you. It's not like you started the fire."

He hadn't. But he hadn't stopped it from bearing down on Sweetheart when he had the chance.

"I hate what happened to this town and the forest surrounding it," he said.

"We all hate it."

"But you weren't on the front lines. I watched the fire consume Sweetheart firsthand. That's why I want to help. You and anyone who wants it. But especially you."

"I don't need help. Yours or anyone's."

"I think you do. You just refuse to admit it."

"I refuse to take your late wife's money." She looked instantly contrite. "Sorry. I shouldn't have snapped at you."

"It's okay." Sam wasn't offended. If anything, he was glad. At least they had gotten to the root of her resistance.

Would she be more willing to accept his help if she learned why his wife had been in that car in the first place and who she was with?

Maybe not. But she might understand what drove him to use the settlement money for good.

THE MARE STOOD PATIENTLY while Annie administered an injection of penicillin. She was less tolerant when Annie inserted the tube of Bute into her mouth, rolling the gooey paste around on her tongue.

"Easy, girl." She stroked the mare's nose. "It tastes bad but will make you feel a lot better."

Together, she and Sam cleaned the mare's mouth and nose. The nasal discharge was clear, which gave Annie hope that the mare was fighting a simple virus and not something more serious. Still, she wouldn't rest easy until the horse was seen by a vet.

"I'll get the mash." Sam left, returning a short while later with a bucket of grain and bran soaked with water and molasses. The delicacy would hopefully tempt the mare to eat and provide necessary hydration.

Annie didn't expect much, not until the Bute kicked in. "You might also try fresh grass instead of hay."

"I'll have Lyndsey pick some after dinner."

"Try adding a cup of salt to her water."

"Where'd you learn that trick?"

"Trial and error and years of nursing sick animals back to health."

To their relief, the mare ate a few mouthfuls of the mash and drank a small amount of salted water. According to Sam, it was more than she'd taken in the past two days.

"Check on her a couple more times before you go to bed. Watch that her breathing doesn't become labored." Annie brushed off her shirt and capris as she exited the stall. "Where do you think my grandmother took off to this time?"

"She's petting the horses." Lyndsey held both Annie and Sam's hands as they went outside.

He sent her a look as if to say, *Kids*.

Yeah, kids.

Granny Orla was at the corrals. Like Annie and her mother, she had once been an accomplished rider. According to the stories, she and her TV-star lover would ride into the mountains and loll away the afternoons at their secret spot. Sam and Annie had followed suit, finding their own secret place.

What to do about Sam? From the second he'd reentered her life, he'd consumed it.

"Thanks for all your help."

"No problem."

Sam walked Annie to her vehicle while Lyndsey went to fetch Granny Orla. Instead, the two of them got involved doling out the carrots that Will kept handy.

"Can I call you if the mare gets worse?" Sam asked.

"There isn't much more I can do."

He caught her wrist before she could open the door. "I should have told you my Hotshot crew was assigned to the fire."

"Yes, you should have."

"I can see you're upset."

"Not upset exactly." The horses were bunched at the corral railing, vying for a treat. Annie watched them as she gathered her thoughts. "It's hard to explain."

"Try."

"It's like I fell from a high cliff and was critically injured. Then I find out you were there at the top, watching the entire time. You even tried to prevent my fall. But you didn't tell me about it, and I have to wonder why."

"I'd give anything to have stopped the fire from reaching Sweetheart."

There was agony in his voice. Sorrow in his eyes. Pain in his heart, deep as her own. She could feel it.

"Wouldn't we all." She lifted her fingers to his cheek.

Not the smartest move. The next moment, she was enveloped in his embrace.

The kiss, gentle and tender, wasn't entirely unexpected. In all honesty, Annie might have prompted it. She would, she decided, give in for a second or two, then disengage herself. Only that didn't happen. She clung to him, letting his mouth settle possessively on hers.

Pure recklessness. And pure heaven.

This was the kind of careless abandonment that had gotten her into trouble with Sam before, when he was a brash young ranch hand and she the local innkeeper's daughter. She'd let herself get carried away…and she was doing it again.

A soft moan escaped her lips, and when his hand pressed firmly into the small of her back, she had the sweet sensation of her bones melting.

He increased his hold on her, but it was she who parted his lips. She who sacrificed control without a care.

She'd missed him.

The realization nearly undid her. He'd been her first love. Her greatest love. And she'd never gotten over him—or the hurt and anger at his abrupt departure.

Those thoughts galvanized her and gave her the strength she needed to resist. Bracing her hands on his shoulders, she pushed away.

"I… We can't." Her complete loss of composure embarrassed her.

Why could he alone have that effect on her?

"The whole time I was married to Trisha, I never forgot about you. About us."

"Not the right thing to say." The reminder of his late wife steadied her.

"Annie, I—"

"You were married. And your wife died in a horrible accident. Please don't dishonor her memory or me by bringing her up seconds after we kissed."

"You're right." He stepped away. The warmth of his body lingered. "But it changes nothing. I want to see you."

"See me? Like a date? No way!"

"Why not?"

She glanced at the corral. Thank goodness for small favors. Granny and Lyndsey were still thoroughly engaged with the horses. "I can give you a hundred reasons."

"There's still a powerful attraction between us. Don't deny it."

She wouldn't. Why bother? He had only to recall their kiss. Correction, kisses. Both occurring with their family members a hundred feet away. This one in broad daylight!

"I have to stay focused on rebuilding the inn and supporting my family. I can't let anything interfere."

No matter how tempting, she added silently.

"One date won't interfere."

As if it would stop there. Look at their past history. Look at the past five minutes.

"Gary wants me to give him more custody of Nessa. He'd probably take her full-time if I let him."

"What! Is he crazy?"

"He's very serious. He's mentioned it enough times that I'm losing sleep at night." She despised the catch in her voice.

"Why would he do that? You're a great mom."

"Because of the apartment."

"It's small but nice. I lived in the back of a horse trailer years ago when I first came here."

"The apartment reminds him too much of the one he grew up in in a not-so-nice part of Vegas. He's also concerned about my grandmother and her bouts with confusion. Also my mother."

"Your mother?"

"You saw her at her best the other night."

"What's her worst?"

"She's depressed."

"I'm no expert but that can't be uncommon after a monumental loss. Hell, half the people in Sweetheart are depressed."

"Half the people in Sweetheart aren't responsible for taking care of Nessa while I'm at work."

"Have you considered delaying the rebuilding and using some of the insurance money to get a larger place?"

"I'd do it in an instant if I could. The problem is there's so little decent available housing in town. We were lucky to get the apartment we did."

"Then Gary's being unreasonable."

She put on a brave smile. "I'm counting on him backing off once we start construction on the inn."

"Let me help you."

"Absolutely not. Gary's my problem to deal with."

"With the inn. Talk to my contractor and architect," he insisted. "What have you got to lose?"

Annie carefully debated the pros and cons. Really, she did have little to lose. And possibly a lot to gain.

"All right, but I refuse to let you cover a dime of their fees. I know you've done that for some people in town."

He grinned broadly. "Chas, the owner of the construction company, is here two or three days a week. The architect will drive up to meet with you."

Annie couldn't believe she was agreeing. For a multitude of good reasons, she'd be wise to keep Sam at arm's length. Yet, a slip of paper appeared in her hand a minute later and she knew without a doubt she'd be calling the numbers on it, grateful to Sam for the referrals.

Chapter Eight

Twenty-four head of horses now resided at the Gold Nugget Ranch, including the pony and the draft mare, nearly recovered from her bout with equine influenza. Dr. Murry had examined her yesterday and set Sam's concerns to rest.

He needed to thank Annie for her help, except he hadn't seen her for three days. Not since giving her the names and numbers of his architect and construction contractor. A casual inquiry placed to both men confirmed she hadn't called them.

Forcing her to accept his assistance wasn't an option. He'd just have to wait her out. Or figure out another way to break through her defenses. So far, animals in need had worked well, but it wouldn't for much longer. Annie was no dummy.

"That fella's a troublemaker." Will referred to their one and only mule, a long-eared, ill-tempered, skinny brown beast who gave all mules a bad name.

"Remind me why we're keeping him," Sam said, fighting hard to hide his exertion. Ten straight minutes of attempting to put a halter on the mule had winded him.

Not Will. "Best pack mule in these parts."

"Hmm." Sam debated offering only short trail rides, ones not requiring extra supplies and provisions carried on a mule's back.

He and Will were in the main corral, attempting to move the entire herd to the newly constructed adjacent corral with its large shade covering. The main corral would soon have a similar covering, if Sam and Will could ever empty it.

The mule stood in the center, glowering at them.

"Come on, you worthless sack of bone," Sam called to him. "Cut us both a break." He wiped his hand across his sweaty brow and turned to Will. "How is it you got all those horses to follow the leader when you unloaded them, and now we can't get one stinking mule through the gate?"

"It's a matter of pride."

"Mine?"

"His." Will inclined his head toward the mule.

Sam might have dismissed his employee's notion that the mule possessed human emotions if it hadn't so far refused a bucket of grain, an apple and sugar cubes. All bribes Sam had tried using to coax the mule into the new corral.

"Let's just leave him for a while. He'll be more cooperative once he misses his buddies."

"Don't count on it."

By now, a sizeable crowd had gathered. In fact, construction had come to a complete standstill. Roofers stopped roofing, painters stopped painting and framers stopped framing. Sam thought he noticed money changing hands and bets being placed.

Even Lyndsey and her new little friend—Irma's middle boy, Gus—abandoned walking the goats in order to watch.

Sam grumbled to himself. No mule was going to best him. Not in front of an audience this size.

"Where you going?" Will called after him.

"To get my rope."

Will's affable chuckle didn't inspire confidence.

Twenty minutes later, all the horses including the mule were in the new corral. Sam's victory wasn't without cost. He had rope burns on his palms, a twisted ankle and a seven-inch tear in his favorite shirt. He was also pretty sure he'd dislocated his left shoulder.

All right, he concluded after rotating it, maybe not dislocated. Just wrenched. He'd be useless tomorrow.

The mule looked no worse for wear. He stood calmly among his brethren in the new corral, his tail swishing at flies.

"What's his name?" All this time, Sam hadn't bothered to ask.

"Make Me. It's short for 'Just Try and Make Me.' That seemed kind of long."

He glared at Will. "You wait till now to tell me that?"

"Won twenty dollars."

"You owe me a beer at least. Let's finish up here and you can take me to the Paydirt and settle up."

"Daddy, Daddy! That was cool." Lyndsey and her pal bounded over. The boy, roughly her age, hadn't left her side since they were introduced earlier that day.

Sam didn't think he had anything to worry about. Yet. Another few years and it might be a different story.

"Yeah, cool." He kneaded his sore shoulder and flexed his twisted ankle. He did not feel cool.

"Gus has been telling me how to take care of the goats."

"You have goats, son?"

"Used to." The boy rolled a pebble back and forth with the toe of his sneaker. "Chickens, too. And a potbelly pig. That was before my mom lost her job."

"Ever take care of baby raccoons?"

"Naw. Raccoons are varmints." At Lyndsey's gasp of horror, he amended his statement. "'Cept for yours."

She scowled at him.

It looked as if Gus had lost some ground.

Sam felt compelled to help the kid. "Seeing as Gus has experience with animals, maybe he could take care of the goats and cat after we go back home. The kits, too. Until they're old enough to be surrendered to the animal sanctuary."

"I don't want him taking care of the animals. I don't want

anybody doing it but me." The higher Lyndsey's voice rose, the more her lower lip trembled.

Sam was grateful the construction workers and Will had returned to their jobs. Fewer witnesses.

"Lyndsey, we've talked about this. We can't take the kits home with us."

"Then let's stay here!"

"We can't. School starts in a month."

"I can go to school with Gus."

Stay here? When did she change her mind? From the very get-go, she hadn't wanted to come to Sweetheart. Except that was before two abandoned kits, two Nubian goats and an ugly-as-sin barn cat entered her life. Oh, and Gus.

"What about Grandpa?"

"He can move here, too."

Sam was thinking how much his own desire to return to California had waned. Reason, however, prevailed. "We have to go home. Grandpa needs us. There's the fall roundup."

"Porky and Daffy will die without me!"

"I'll take care of them," Gus offered. "Even if they are varmints."

Sam was marginally glad to see he wasn't the only male in the vicinity saying completely the wrong thing.

With an anguished cry, Lyndsey ran into the house. Sam imagined her running up the stairs to her bedroom and slamming the door shut.

Gus sighed. "Women."

Sam didn't think he'd ever be concurring with an eight-year-old.

They found Gus's mother in the kitchen. She confirmed Lyndsey was in her room.

Sam went upstairs and knocked on her closed bedroom door. "Sweetie."

He heard muffled thumping noises from within but no invitation to enter.

"Gus is looking for you."

"I don't want to talk to him. Or you."

Sam hesitated before heading back down the stairs. They'd been through this exact same scenario often since Trisha's death. Lyndsey would sequester herself and refuse to talk to him or anybody until she was ready.

"Irma, you mind keeping an eye on her for me?" Sam asked. "I'm heading into town with Will."

"Not at all."

Gus sat glumly at the long oak table.

"You might as well go outside and play, son."

"I'll wait for her."

He would? Sam wasn't sure how he felt about that.

Behind the barn, Sam discovered Will repairing the same antique buggy that had sat in front of the ranch for decades. Will thought it would be a nice touch for the guests, and Sam agreed.

"You ready to buy me that beer?"

"It's not quitting time yet."

"I need a break. We're taking the rest of the afternoon off."

"You're the boss." Will straightened and deposited the wrench he'd been using into the open toolbox. "Want me to drive?"

"The hell with driving. Let's ride. I haven't seen these mountains from the back of a horse for nine years."

The hills surrounding the Gold Nugget were lush and green, deep in the throes of summer splendor. Birds flitted from one thick Ponderosa Pine bough to another as Sam and Will rode by. Squirrels scampered into hiding. Faces of cows peeked out from behind brush, the grazing stock of some nearby rancher.

Sam relaxed, settling into the rhythmic sway of the horse's easy gait. For a while, he forgot about his troubles and, in this untainted stretch of wilderness, all about the fire.

Then, he and Will crested the next rise. In the valley below lay Sweetheart.

What was left of it.

Strips, some a quarter mile wide and black as coal, crisscrossed the town and continued up the opposing mountain, marking the fire's descent from Cohea Ridge. The place where Sam had been that day, watching in horror and frustration as the wind changed direction.

"Pretty bad, huh?" Will said thoughtfully.

Pretty bad didn't begin to describe it. Fate had dealt this place and its people a terrible blow.

Sam almost turned back around.

Riding through town was equally disheartening. The horses plodded slowly along, giving Sam plenty of opportunity to study the devastation in detail. By the time he and Will reached the saloon, his spirits were low and his determination wavering. He needed more than a beer to erase the images seared in his memory.

The fire had divided countless times as it burned through Sweetheart, attacking some homes and buildings and leaving others to stand alone like tiny islands in a sea of blackness.

So much devastation. Would converting the Gold Nugget into a working guest ranch be enough to revitalize Sweetheart? Doubts crept in and anchored.

Sam and Will tethered their horses to the hitching rail behind the building and went inside. The mayor's bar and grill was the only local watering hole in Sweetheart to survive. Two others had succumbed to the fire, another to a lack of honeymooners and tourists. As a result, the Paydirt was typically crowded most evenings and weekends.

Mayor Dempsey was behind the bar, busily serving drinks with the help of her brother-in-law, who was also on the town council.

Ever since the first Dempseys settled in the area, one or more of them had continually held positions of prominence and authority. Last election, the tradition continued when the mayor's nephew was elected sheriff.

Annie's family and their inn might have been the heart of Sweetheart, but the Dempsey family was the muscle.

"Welcome, gentlemen." The mayor flashed Sam and Will a broad smile as they approached the bar and placed their orders. "Been a while since we've had a couple of young, handsome cowboys ride up on their horses. Reminds me of the old days."

Sam would have selected a table, but Will sidled over to the last stool at the bar and plunked down, giving Sam the impression this was his employee's regular seat. The stool next to Will was vacant, and Sam took it.

When Will attempted to pay for the beers, the mayor refused him.

"For you, Sam, drinks are on the house. And your hired hand."

"I can't accept that."

"Sure you can. With everything you're doing for this town, the jobs you've given folks, the business your guest ranch will bring in, I wouldn't think of charging you."

As if on cue, a cement truck chugged noisily down the street outside the bar, its hydraulic brakes squealing as it slowed.

"Think the horses are okay?" Sam asked.

Will shrugged, and then nodded. "If they get scared and run off, they won't go far."

"Won't go far" could be all the way back to the Gold Nugget.

"Look at that," the mayor gushed. "Third truck this hour. Heading to the Abramses' shop to pour their foundation."

Sam was acquainted with the Abramses. They were one of the families who'd taken him up on his offer to assist with their reconstruction costs. He was glad to see work had started.

"If not for you, the Abramses would have moved," the mayor continued. "Now they're staying."

"Hear, hear." A patron sitting down the bar from Sam raised his glass in salute.

The knot twisting Sam's stomach eased slightly.

Not long after, another truck passed, this one bearing the logo of a lumber company from Lake Tahoe. A small cheer went up throughout the saloon and another toast was made to Sam. The mayor declared a round of drinks for the house.

Sam's only regret was that the trucks weren't en route to Annie's inn. Why hadn't she contacted his contractor or the architect?

Maybe he should have *them* call *her*. No, that would be interfering, and Annie wouldn't like it. Any assistance she accepted from him—even something as simple as a referral—had to be on her own terms.

He wasn't convinced rebuilding the inn was the best course of action for her, but if that was what she truly wanted, needed, he'd stand behind her.

Not an hour passed that he didn't think about their kisses and recall the taste of her mouth. The sensation of her going pliant in his arms. The stirrings inside him that she triggered with just a glance or a smile.

It was more than lust or longing. He could admit to himself he hadn't ever really fallen out of love with her, and with a little push, he'd be right back where he was nine years ago.

Where would that leave them? Leave him? Annie didn't appear to be teetering on the edge like he was.

Rousing himself, he drained half his beer. The good thing about keeping company with Will was that the man didn't talk much and appreciated that same quality in others.

At another loud cheer from the patrons, Sam turned sideways to look out the window, expecting to see another truck passing by.

To his surprise and delight, Annie had walked into the saloon. He automatically started to rise as she made her way toward him.

Will also stood and tugged on the brim of his cowboy hat in greeting. "Later," he said to Sam and found a vacant chair farther down the bar.

Sam didn't stop him. He wanted some time alone with Annie and hoped she was here to discuss starting construction on the inn.

Right. He really hoped she was here to see him.

"Hi." Her manner was reserved. "I saw your horses and hoped you might be here."

She recognized his horses? The thought gave Sam a small surge of pleasure. She was paying attention to him.

"Can I buy you a beer?" He gestured to the stool Will had vacated.

"No, thanks. I rarely drink since Nessa was born. Besides, I'm not staying."

She'd hardly finished her sentence when the mayor slid an icy soda in front of her with an "On the house."

Sam made a mental note to leave a sizeable tip before leaving. "Did you need something?" he asked.

"I do." She sat down and took a sip of her soda as if requiring fortification. "Can you come outside with me for a minute?"

"Sure." He motioned to Will that he'd be right back and went with Annie.

She took him to her SUV and opened the rear hatch. Inside the cargo area was a large cardboard shipping box.

"What is it?" Sam peered curiously at the box.

"I found this today. At the base of an aspen tree. We were assisting a team of scientists from the University of Nevada, collecting density readings near Cohea Ridge."

She carefully opened the top of the box, just enough for Sam to see in.

A large bird huddled in the corner and eyed them with insolence and suspicion.

"It's a goshawk," Annie said. "I'm not sure what happened to him, but he's pretty beat-up. Could be he got in a fight with a larger bird of prey over food. The supply of rodents has drastically dwindled. Or, it's possible some other predator tried to make a meal of him."

"That's too bad. He's a beautiful bird."

The hawk sported thick white stripes over each gleaming eye, without a doubt its most prominent feature next to its hooked beak. The wings were tucked close to its body. Unfurled, Sam estimated they would span more than three feet.

"I was hoping you could help."

"With what?"

"Keep him. Rehabilitate him. Until he's ready to be released back into the wild. I'd do it myself, but my landlord won't allow it. And Lyndsey's so good with animals."

The last thing Sam wanted or needed was another animal for his daughter to foster. She was already too attached to the ones they had. Just look at their earlier blowup over the suggestion that Gus assume responsibility for their brood when they returned to California. And hawks required more specialized care than baby raccoons, goats and a stray cat. He knew that from the times he'd helped Annie with the various birds she'd rescued.

"Annie…"

"Please."

The desperation in her voice turned his resolve to mush. "On one condition."

"Name it," she answered without reservation.

"Come back inside. Finish your soda."

"But the hawk—"

"Will be fine for a little while longer. In fact, he's probably a lot better off and safer in the box than the woods. After dinner, you can meet me at the Gold Nugget. Bring Nessa.

Bring your whole family if you want. While Nessa rides the pony, you and I can get this fellow situated."

After a brief hesitation, Annie closed the lid on the box and shut the rear hatch on her SUV. "Thirty minutes. No more."

Not much time. Sam would have to work fast.

Chapter Nine

Annie shouldn't have agreed to Sam's request. She should have insisted they go straight to the Gold Nugget. No bringing the family. No pony ride.

Of course, going *straight* there would have been difficult, considering his mode of transportation was horseback. And if she'd refused, he might not have agreed to foster the hawk.

With little choice, she found herself sitting at a table in the Paydirt with him.

Visiting the ranch, conversing with Sam, was becoming a habit. One she didn't seem capable of breaking. One she possibly didn't want to break.

"If you're wondering why I haven't called your architect and contractor yet, I've been busy with work."

"I wasn't wondering."

"Oh." Then why insist they talk?

He appeared far more relaxed than she felt, with his long legs stretched out, his cowboy hat pushed back on his head and one forearm propped casually on the table.

She, on the other hand, couldn't sit still and continuously stirred the ice in her soda with her straw.

"I owe you an explanation," he said.

"For what?"

"Why I didn't tell you about my crew being called to the

fire. I wasn't sure what to say, so I said nothing. Not the right thing to do."

"I would have liked to know, yeah." Also that he was returning to Sweetheart and buying the Gold Nugget. If only to prepare herself. "In the end, it doesn't make any difference."

"It actually does. And here's where things get sticky."

"I don't follow."

No longer relaxed, Sam sat up and drained the last of the beer he'd been nursing. After that, he took several seconds to collect himself.

"You remember how the wind suddenly changed direction, sending the fire toward Sweetheart?"

"How could I not? One minute the officials were telling us we were safe. The next, we had two hours to evacuate. Even then, they assured us it was simply a precaution. Ten hours later, the town was a raging inferno."

If Sam gripped his empty beer bottle any tighter, he'd shatter it.

"Are you okay?" she asked.

"No."

He was beginning to alarm her.

"What's wrong?"

His face was flushed and his brow damp. She leaned forward, tempted to place her palm on his forehead and test for a fever.

"I knew the wind was going to change direction from west to south before it did."

"I don't understand."

"I've been a volunteer Hotshot for a lot of years. It gets to where you have a sixth sense, more accurate than all the scientific equipment and experts put together. I've been right more times than I've been wrong. My gut was working overtime that day, telling me Sweetheart was in danger."

Annie sat slowly back in her chair, Sam's revelation sending a shock wave pulsing through her. "Why didn't you do something?"

"I did. I radioed my commander. Insisted crews be moved from the line we were holding on the west perimeter of the fire to the south perimeter."

"He ignored your warning?"

"Just the opposite. He's worked with me a lot of summers and trusts me. So he relayed my information to Fire Camp."

She could see the outcome in his eyes. "They didn't listen."

"The chief instructed us to hold steady. All the reports and scientific data indicated weather conditions were going to remain stable. The wind would continue blowing in a westerly direction."

"But it didn't."

"No."

The emotion in that single word brought tears to Annie's eyes. Sam was in pain. She was in pain. Her town, her inn, might have been spared.

"Why didn't you disobey orders?" She wasn't criticizing him, only attempting to understand.

"I've asked myself that question a thousand times a day, and the answer comes back the same. I don't know. We're trained to obey orders, and I could have been suspended. Terminated. But that's just an excuse." His voice was hoarse, as if he'd been screaming for hours without rest.

Had it been like that the day of the fire? Had he screamed until his throat was raw?

"Could you have saved Sweetheart? If you disobeyed orders?"

"Not without backup. My crew consisted of nineteen men. There were two other crews in that section. Together, maybe we could have stopped the fire. Slowed it down for sure until reinforcements arrived."

"Only if your crew and the others agreed to disobey orders, too."

"Yeah."

"What were the chances of that?"

"We won't ever know. That's what I have to live with."

"Yes, we do know, Sam. I see the aftermath of that fire every time I look out my window or drive down the street. I also work for the NDF and experience firsthand what that fire did every day on the job. A handful of Hotshots battling a two-mile raging inferno would be like sending a single guy with a garden hose to extinguish a burning building."

"I should have tried harder. Talked to the chief myself instead of leaving it up to my commanding offi—"

"Nobody died."

He looked at her in confusion.

"The fire was the largest and most destructive one this state has seen in years. The damage to wilderness and property is immeasurable. But nobody died. And there were very few injuries. Most of them minor. Sweetheart was the only town to sustain any damage. It could have been a lot worse. You've seen worse in some of the fires you've fought."

"I have. But those towns weren't places where I'd lived. The residents weren't people I knew and cared about. There wasn't a special woman who once meant the world to me."

She reached for his hand. His large, strong fingers curled instantly around hers. When he applied a slight pressure, she returned it.

"You don't have to beat yourself up with guilt, Sam. We live in the Sierra Nevada. Winds constantly change direction with no warning. It's nature."

"I could have done more."

"You and the other Hotshots gave us enough time to evacuate the entire town. Your warning made those scientists and personnel in charge take a closer look at protocol. Reevaluate it."

"I'm not sure about that."

Maybe he wasn't, but some of the tension drained from him.

"I know you came back to help. Because of guilt. Only the fire isn't your burden to bear, and you're not solely responsible for Sweetheart's recovery."

His smile, though faint, was the first one since they'd come back inside the Paydirt. "I'd still like to try."

Annie suddenly remembered the time. She really should get home. Nessa would be waiting for her, their dinner getting cold. Before the fire, her mother would have been impatiently waiting, too. She'd always been a stickler about how and when her food was served, right down to the china plates and crystal salt-and-pepper shakers.

Now, most of her efforts were centered on making it through the day.

Annie realized that other than seeing Nessa, she had no interest in returning to the apartment. It was a small, dreary and discouraging place. She'd much rather be sitting here with Sam.

"Whatever your motives, people are grateful." She removed her hand from his and resumed stirring her soda. "Can I ask you a personal question?"

"Sure."

"Why are you using the settlement money from your wife's accident to cover the contractor's profit? Shouldn't that money go to Lyndsey? Not that it's any of my business."

"I want some good to come out of Trisha's accident."

"You're spending money on people you hardly know. On a ranch you probably bought strictly for sentimental reasons."

"Spontaneous or not, buying the Gold Nugget was the right decision. I want this town to thrive again. I want to see couples walking hand in hand on their way to the chapel. I want your inn to be the heart of Sweetheart."

Her smile softened. "Is that a hint to call your architect and contractor?"

"Might be."

"I'll do it. Tomorrow. I promise." And not leave the task

to her mother. "But what about Lyndsey? It's not fair she lose her share of the money."

Annie had hesitated before speaking. Sam didn't when he responded.

"The settlement was large. Significant. The drunk driver who hit Trisha was well-off and his level of intoxication far exceeded the legal limit. He's currently imprisoned for two felony counts of vehicular manslaughter. Even without the settlement, Lyndsey's well taken care of. My father-in-law intends to leave the ranch to her. Trisha was his only child and Lyndsey's his only grandchild."

Something Sam said stopped Annie. "*Two* counts of manslaughter?"

"Trisha wasn't alone in the car."

"How terrible." Annie released a shuddering sigh. What if Lyndsey had been the other occupant? Imagining it gave her chills. "Her friend's family must be devastated."

"They are. His wife had no idea he was cheating on her with Trisha. Just like I had no idea."

"Cheating!" Poor Sam. What a blow that must have been. "Are you sure they were lovers? They could have been acquaintances or business associates."

Annie had no reason to defend Sam's late wife, but he was obviously suffering, and she longed to ease his grief.

"I'm sure. Trisha and her lover were returning from an afternoon together when they were struck." He resumed choking his empty beer bottle. "She died almost instantly. Massive internal injuries. Her lover lived an hour. Long enough to make a deathbed confession. It damn near killed me. His wife took it worse."

It seemed to Annie as if Sam had taken it pretty bad himself.

She understood his marriage might not have been made in heaven, and she was certainly no one to judge. Not with her track record. His resentment, however, sounded more serious.

"Trisha would have wanted the settlement money to go to Lyndsey and you," she said.

"I won't take a dime of it."

"She had feelings for you."

"I doubt it." He bit out the words. "She rarely thought of anyone besides herself. If she had, she wouldn't have been in that car in the first place."

"I'm so sorry. That must have been…" Annie started to say *unbearable* only to realize how inadequately that described what he must have gone through. "Does Lyndsey know?"

"She doesn't. And I may never tell her. I see no reason to taint the memory of her mother.

Neither did Annie. Not at eight years old. "She may find out when she's older. Family members could talk. There was probably news coverage. If she eventually decides that she needs closure, she may investigate the accident."

"Maybe."

Annie was in no position to advise Sam on how to handle that day if it ever came. She only hoped he'd be ready.

Someday, certainly before *she* was ready, Nessa would inquire about her parents' divorce and what went wrong. Annie prayed she'd say the right thing.

All at once, she wanted to go home and hold her baby in her arms. It didn't seem polite, running off seconds after Sam had revealed such personal and private information.

"If there's anything I can do for you or Lyndsey, don't hesitate to ask."

"Just help find homes for all these critters she's collecting."

"And I've made your problem bigger by foisting a goshawk on you."

"I don't mind."

She didn't think he did. His voice had lost its rough edge. "You're a good man, Sam."

In answer, his gaze traveled her face, long and lingeringly.

Her cheeks warmed under his intense scrutiny, but she didn't look away.

"Can I get you a refill?" The mayor interrupted them, a drink tray balanced on her arm.

Annie glanced around the bar, and her worst fears were confirmed when a half-dozen heads quickly turned away.

"No, thanks." Annie brushed self-consciously at her hair. "People are staring at us," she said after the mayor moved to the next table.

"They've see it before." Sam's grin wasn't the least bit contrite.

"Not recently. And not again. I don't want them or you getting the wrong idea."

"Too late, girl. I've been getting wrong ideas since that first kiss. Actually, since the first day I saw you at the Gold Nugget. Standing at the bottom of the stairs."

She nearly groaned with frustration—and would have if not for Sam's guaranteed amusement.

"I'd better hurry." She scooted back from the table. "I'll be by around seven with Nessa and the hawk. I was thinking we could put him in that old chicken coop next to the barn."

"Will and I will have it cleaned out before you get there. Patch any holes."

He walked her outside to her SUV. His horses weren't the only ones to be tethered behind the Paydirt Saloon, but it had been a while. The familiar scene gave Annie a cozy feeling inside. In this one small way, life was returning to normal.

"I really will call the architect and contractor tomorrow."

"Let me know how that goes."

He propped an arm on the roof of her vehicle, beside her open door, his stance the same pure male one that he'd assumed the other day.

Annie's resistance, never all that strong where Sam was concerned, weakened. Of its own volition, her body swayed toward his.

How many faces were pressed to the bar's windows? How many pairs of eyes were peering at them? She didn't dare look. She didn't really care.

"Better hurry," he murmured lazily, "if Nessa's going to ride that pony. It gets dark by eight."

"Yeah." Annie moved…marginally closer to Sam rather than away, convinced she'd lost her mind. "She'll be really disappointed if we're late."

One minute. Two minutes. What would it hurt? She lifted her face to Sam's.

At the same moment that his head dipped to claim the kiss she offered, a vehicle hauled into the parking lot and came to a tire-squealing stop. Right next to her SUV. Too loud and too close to ignore.

Annie reeled, ready to give the driver a warning.

The van, with the distinctive Dempsey General Store and Trading Post logo painted on the side, was one of a kind.

The door opened, and Gary emerged. He approached Annie and Sam, his gait purposeful and an angry scowl on his face.

Chapter Ten

"Gary, what's wrong?" As Annie rushed forward to meet him, she noticed Nessa sat in the van's passenger seat. Not Linda Lee. Her concern spiked to alarm. "Why do you have Nessa?"

"Can we talk?" He fired a decidedly unfriendly glance in Sam's direction. "In private."

Not answering, she tried to skirt him. "Is she all right?"

He restrained her with a hand on her arm. "She's fine. Which is fortunate."

Her heart verged on exploding. Through the window, Nessa appeared safe and secure in her car seat, happily reading a picture book. Seeing her didn't calm Annie.

"What's going on?" she demanded.

"I went to the apartment," Gary explained, pulling her aside. "She'd left her Barbie dolls at my place, and I thought I'd drop them off. When I got there, she answered the door. A three-year-old. Not your mom or grandmother. And the door wasn't locked. With all the construction going on and testing in the mountains, this town is full of strangers."

Guilt and horror instantly consumed Annie. "Where was Mom?"

"Asleep. I went through the apartment and found her in bed."

"I'll talk to her again."

"You don't get it, Annie. Nessa was playing unsupervised.

In the kitchen. Where there's a gas stove. And your mom was dead to the world. Took a full minute of shaking to wake her."

The part of Annie's mind clinging to reason argued that sleeping wasn't so terrible. She'd occasionally lie down for a brief rest while her mother or grandmother watched Nessa. Not, however, when she and Nessa were alone. Then, she'd coax Nessa to lie down with her.

"And your grandmother had taken off again. Who knows where? She must have left the front door unlocked." Gary's tone was grim. "Annie, anybody could have walked right in and snatched Nessa. Or, she could have wandered off and gotten into all kinds of trouble. Lost. Hit by a car."

She had no excuse. "Gary, I… It won't happen again."

"I was going to find you, talk to you. See if we couldn't figure out other day care. I get that you have to work, but there must be more reliable resources in town." His concern for Nessa was genuine. "Except here you are, having a drink with your old boyfriend while our daughter's in danger." Another accusatory glance at Sam.

"It was a soda."

"You should have been home. With Nessa. She's your first priority."

He was right. At the very least, she should have called her mother before stopping at the Paydirt. The ringing phone would have woken her up.

But she'd been preoccupied. Talking to Sam. Holding his hand. Gazing into his face. Vying for a kiss.

Oh, God. She was the worst mother ever.

"It won't happen again, Gary. I swear to you." She made another attempt to squeeze past him.

He wouldn't allow it.

"Let me see Nessa!"

"Not yet." Was he angrier about her mother sleeping when she should have been watching Nessa or that Annie was with Sam?

"You have no right to keep me from her."

"I have the right to expect my child is safely supervised when I'm not there. It's also my responsibility to see that she's living in decent housing."

"The apartment's fine."

"It's small and crowded. She doesn't have to live that way. Not when I have plenty of room at my house."

"Sweetheart isn't anything like where you grew up."

His tone softened. "I'm not trying to take her away from you. I only want to provide for her as best I can."

He might not think he was trying to take Nessa away from Annie, but that's sure what it sounded like. "I'm seeing my daughter now," she said sternly.

"I think it's best I take Nessa home with me tonight."

"The hell you are!"

"Stop by after you get off work. We'll make some decisions."

Anger dissolved into pleading. "We have an agreement. Don't use Nessa to punish me."

All at once, Sam's arm stretched out and made contact with Gary's chest. Annie was unaware he'd moved to stand beside her.

"Let Annie see her daughter."

"This is none of your concern, Wyler." Gary didn't budge. "Butt out."

"I'll butt out when Annie tells me to."

She didn't. While Sam and Gary stood arguing, she ducked by them and ran to Gary's van. Hands shaking, she removed Nessa and the Barbie dolls and loaded them into the SUV's rear seat, opening several windows for ventilation. Only then did Sam lower his arm, releasing Gary. Her ex-husband was none too happy.

When Nessa was secure and assured everything was well, that Mommy and Daddy were just talking, Annie returned to the two men and braced herself for Gary's onslaught.

"I'll expect you promptly after work."

"I'll see you Friday when it's your turn with Nessa."

"You either come by tomorrow or my attorney will be in touch. That's a promise. Our daughter deserves better, and she's going to get it."

"EASY NOW, I'VE got you."

"Let me go."

Sam held Annie, refusing to release her until her shaking subsided.

"Gary's gone. Everything's fine."

"No, it's not."

The anguish in her voice ripped him in two. "Nothing bad happened, Annie."

"Gary's coming after me for full custody."

"He was mad at me and taking it out on you." Sam stroked her back. "He'll get over it."

"He's threatened before."

"Do you really think he was serious?" That was bothersome. Sam had assumed Gary was simply reacting out of anger or being pressured by his wife. Nice as the woman had been to him, it was obvious she had a grudge against Annie. "You're Nessa's mother. There is no way a judge will grant him full custody just because one time your mom happened to fall asleep and your grandmother left the front door unlocked. Especially when Nessa wasn't hurt."

"He can still make trouble for me," she said unevenly, her glance going to Nessa in the SUV's rear seat. The girl was happily occupied with the dolls Gary had returned. "Between my mom's depression and my grandmother's episodes of confusion, he has a strong case. God, I'd give anything to move."

"Let me ask my real estate agent. She may have some strings she can pull."

"Worth a try, I suppose."

To Sam's disappointment, Annie disengaged herself from his embrace. "I really need to get home. I don't want Gary telling the judge that I stand in front of bars with men while our daughter is forced to wait inside my vehicle." After one step, she paused and pressed a hand to her forehead. "I forgot about the goshawk."

"I'll take care of him."

"How will you get him home? You're riding a horse."

He nodded toward the door of the Paydirt. "I'll catch a lift with someone inside. Will can ride his horse home and lead mine."

"Are you sure?"

"Get a move on and quit worrying."

"I'll stop by tomorrow."

"No rush. Whenever's convenient for you. I learned enough from helping you out with your bird rescues—I can manage to take care of this fellow for a few days without killing him."

"Sam!"

"That was a joke."

She tried to smile, but the attempt failed. "Call me."

"I will. You just concentrate on yourself and your family."

"And on finding alternative day care."

"I have something that might help in the meantime."

"Oh, you're starting a day care center at the ranch now?"

"No, but that's not a bad idea. For the guests."

"Be serious, Sam."

"Okay, I was joking again. A little."

This time a smile broke through. "You've done so much for me already."

Was she including the hug? "If you need help searching for your grandmother, let me know."

"Hopefully, she's at the neighbors' and not the inn ruins."

"Or on her way to the Gold Nugget."

"Right." She opened the driver's side door and asked Nessa, "You hungry, sweetie pie? We'll leave in just a minute. I have to give Mr. Wyler something."

They went to the rear of the vehicle and lifted the hatch.

"I'll have my construction contractor send over an installer tomorrow. When's a good time?"

"Installer for what?" she asked, reaching for the cardboard box and peeking inside. The goshawk hadn't moved.

"A door alarm."

"A what?"

"Individual sensors for doors," Sam answered. "I ordered a few for the ranch. They're like a mini alarm system. When the door's opened, a buzzer sounds. Loud enough to be heard from a hundred feet away. The contractor recommended them to deter guests from going where they shouldn't, like the tool shed or tack room. If your mother were to fall asleep again, the buzzer would wake her."

She paused, hand on the box. "I can't let you do that."

"You can, and you will. For Nessa and your grandmother. And for your peace of mind. You don't need to be worrying about your family all day when you're at work."

"It would show Gary that I'm committed," she said, relenting.

Sam allowed himself a moment's satisfaction. Little by little, he was breaking down her resistance.

"The installer will call your mom and give her a heads-up on his arrival time."

"I insist on paying you." She blinked what might be tears from her eyes.

"Okay, but I'm giving you a smoking deal."

Unable to resist, he reached out and cradled her cheek. She leaned into his palm, covering his hand with hers. They stood like that for several seconds. In some ways, the gesture was more intimate than their recent kisses.

She withdrew slowly. "I wouldn't be surprised if Gary's parked down the road, waiting for me."

Sam remained where he was, holding the box with the goshawk, until her vehicle disappeared behind the bend. Inside the Paydirt, he conferred with Will about the horses and hitched a ride back to the Gold Nugget with Emmett, the ranch's former caretaker. While the old man talked, Sam thought of other ways he could help Annie besides the door alarm.

Something about her day-care comment stuck. Not that he would seriously consider starting one. But Irma frequently brought one or two of her brood with her, and it didn't seem to cause any problems. The opposite was true, if anything. Lyndsey loved having playmates.

There was no reason Fiona couldn't bring Nessa to the ranch, too. And, as long as Fiona was there, she might be willing to pitch in.

Sam needed a guest-relations manager, one with experience. Fiona fit the bill better than anyone else in Sweetheart.

The more he considered offering Annie's mother a job, the more the idea appealed to him. And with Fiona and Nessa at the ranch, Annie might be inclined to stop by more often.

It was, he decided confidently, a win-win for everyone.

ANNIE SAT AT the stoplight and replayed the cryptic voice-mail message on her cell phone for a third time. Her mother sounded happy. Like her old self. That might have given Annie comfort if not for the message itself. She'd been concerned enough to leave work an hour early and drive to the Gold Nugget, where her mother was—this part really didn't make sense—employed.

Sam must have invited Nessa out for another pony ride, to make up for the one they'd missed the other day after the run-in with Gary. Annie's mother had merely gotten her words jumbled.

The light turned green and Annie accelerated, unable to shake the concern that had plagued her since she'd checked her messages while on afternoon break.

What could be wrong?

Nothing, she assured herself. Besides, this would give her

an opportunity to see the goshawk and rest easy knowing it was being properly cared for.

She passed the inn, what was left of it. She had no choice. This road was the only one leading north out of town and to the ranch.

A hundred yards separated the inn from its closest neighbors on either side. Like the inn, the ice cream shop to the right had been burned to the ground. Luckily, the wedding chapel to the left, with its quaint rose gardens and pine gazebo, had escaped.

Sadly, all the weddings scheduled to take place in the gardens had been cancelled, the couples forced to choose other locations. Annie indulged herself, reminiscing about life before the fire.

Nearly every day, at almost any hour, she could pass by the chapel and catch sight of a ceremony in progress. Many of those couples, young, old and in between, strolled across the adjoining lawns to the inn, where they would begin their honeymoon.

Being a small part of such a big moment had brought joy to Annie, her mother and grandmother. So much, they'd dedicated their lives to it. She wanted that to happen again. To participate in people's happily-ever-afters. It was the driving force behind her rebuilding her family's legacy.

And silly as it may be, she believed her own happily-ever-after was also tied to rebuilding.

Annie wasn't sure how much longer the chapel owners could hang on. Their minister, a spry and delightful retiree, had moved away last week to live with his daughter in Utah.

On a positive note, she mused as she drove on, to her, Sweetheart was looking less and less like a ghost town. Nearly a third of the damaged homes had been repaired or restored. Another third were under construction, several of those thanks to Sam. The businesses, however, were another story. With no honeymooners and tourists booked, the owners saw no point in hurrying.

The opening of the Gold Nugget might change their minds. Except what would happen to all the wedding businesses if the returning tourists were only interested in the cowboy experience, as Sam put it, and not getting married?

She was half tempted to stop at the inn, check if there were any more treasures to unearth. Definitely not the book Granny Orla had been asking about the other day.

With a start, she realized she hadn't visited the site in nearly two weeks. Not since the day Sam had returned. When had her daily habit stopped, and why hadn't she noticed?

At the next corner, Wanda DeMarco flagged her down. Annie pulled to a stop and lowered the passenger window.

"Hey, Annie." The grade-school teacher grappled with a large plastic crate.

Wanda was both blessed and cursed. Though she'd lost some of her students when their parents moved, school would start next month, right on schedule. Unfortunately, her home had sustained severe damage, and she'd been forced to move in with a fellow teacher.

"Need a lift somewhere?" Annie asked, leaning across the seat toward the open window.

"I'm fine. This isn't as heavy as it looks. And I'm just going over to the chapel."

"You sure?" The crate did look heavy, and Wanda's ample bosom was heaving with strain.

"Trust me, I need the exercise. Hey, listen, you have some items from the inn you've found, right?"

"A few."

"If you need a place to store them, the Yeungs have opened up the chapel's basement. That's where I'm taking these quilts. My great-great-great-grandmother brought them from Illinois when she and her husband traveled cross-country by wagon train." She hugged the crate closer. "I'm so grateful

I got them out before the fire and that I have a place to store them until we rebuild."

"Most everything I've found from the inn is small."

"Well, just in case." Wanda's pudgy face glowed. "There's quite a collection accumulating. I swear, you look around that basement, and it's like seeing the entire history of Sweetheart all in one place. You should drop by."

Annie didn't know if her heart could take it. Too many bittersweet memories. Even so, she said, "Maybe I will. If you're sure I can't give you a lift—"

"Absolutely not. See you later."

"Wait, Wanda. Do you know of anyone offering day care?"

"Not off the top of my head. But you might call the school office. They keep a list of certified day care operators."

"Thanks for the tip."

Annie found herself gawking as she pulled into the ranch. Despite it having been only a few days, the changes were numerous.

The bunkhouse/guest rooms appeared finished, at least from the outside. The new flowerbeds flanking the front steps and the deep green shutters on the windows were a nice touch. The addition to the old barn had been framed, and the workers were starting on the siding and the roof. The exterior walls of an entirely new building had been constructed near the horse corrals. Annie assumed the building would house the tack room Sam had mentioned and possibly an office. The ancient barbed-wire fence surrounding the pasture behind the barn had been removed and replaced with a five-foot sucker rod fence, forming the temporary arena.

A small thrill of excitement coursed through her. It was really happening. Before long, Sam would have a fully functional guest ranch. And people would return to Sweetheart. She could think of nothing more wonderful.

Parking in front of the house next to her mother's sedan, she walked briskly to the front porch, smiling and nodding to the workers she passed. More than one she recognized as locals. Sam probably had no trouble finding extra laborers from the overflowing ranks of Sweetheart's unemployed.

Annie's intention was to locate Irma and ask where she could find her mother and Nessa. She wasn't expecting to discover Nessa and Irma's youngest playing on the parlor floor.

"Mommy, hi!" Nessa shot up and skipped over to Annie, giving her a hug.

"Sweetie pie, where's Grandma?"

Nessa ignored the question. "We're playing animal hospital."

A veritable zoo of stuffed toys was strewn across the hardwood floor, some "patients" swaddled in dish towels, other sporting toilet-paper bandages.

"That's nice. Mommy's going to find Grandma."

In the kitchen, Annie was greeted with a "You're here!" as her mother and Irma emerged from the walk-in pantry, Irma looking tall and ungainly next to petite Fiona.

"Mom, what's going on? I didn't understand your message."

"Sam offered me a job. As guest-relations manager." Her mother stood straighter. "I accepted."

"Wh-when did this happen?"

"Today. He said I could start tomorrow, but I decided to get a jump on things."

"Just like that?" Annie barely noticed Irma depositing her load on the counter.

"I didn't need any time to think about it. The pay is good, the hours reasonable, the benefits generous." She smiled at Irma. "I like the staff."

"Mom, you can't just take a job without talking to me first."

Fiona's smile waned. "I wasn't aware I required your permission."

"What about Nessa? And Granny Orla?" Annie was thinking she'd need adult day care now as well as child care.

"Sam said they can come here for the meantime."

"You can't do your job and watch them." Her mother could barely maintain their small apartment while supervising the energetic and wily pair. Look what had happened a few days ago when Gary showed up unexpectedly.

"We thought we'd take turns," Irma interjected. "And there's my oldest. Carrie's in charge of the laundry. She can also babysit the kids. Until school starts, anyway."

Annie's head started to swim. "This makes no sense."

"It's only temporary," her mother assured her.

"Nessa and Granny Orla staying here while you work or the job?"

"Annie, we do what we have to. Right now, I need a job and we need the money."

She didn't stop to think how alive and engaged her mother appeared and how much vitality she exuded. Neither did she consider how necessary the extra income was. All she felt was the betrayal, like a spear to her heart.

Her mother had taken a job, made a decision that greatly affected Annie and Nessa and done it without talking to Annie first. Like Gary and the preschool. Did no one think her capable of caring for her child?

Annie glanced around the kitchen. "Where's Sam?"

"Last I knew he was in the barn."

"Keep an eye on Nessa for me. I won't be long."

"Darling, please."

Ignoring her mother, Annie kissed the top of her daughter's head on her way through the parlor, left the house and hastily covered the grounds to the barn in search of Sam. He shouldn't have offered her mother the job without discussing it with her first, and she was going to let him know that in no uncertain terms.

Chapter Eleven

Sam wasn't where she expected to find him, which was with the raccoon kits. Rather, he, Lyndsey and Irma's son Gus were at the chicken coop beside the barn. The coop holding the goshawk Annie had asked Sam to foster.

The kids crowded around him, watching him repair a hole in the coop door. As she neared, Annie realized Sam was actually instructing Lyndsey and Gus on how to hammer a nail. The two appeared to be taking turns. Cute and charming and typical Sam.

Once again, her anger at him dissipated. Well, not entirely. She was still going to give him a piece of her mind. Just with less vehemence.

Wrapped up in her thoughts, she almost tripped over the stray cat. It crouched on all fours in the high grass, tail twitching as it stared intently at the goshawk. The hawk, perched atop a stripped ponderosa branch inside the coop, was more interested in the humans and their loud banging.

Narrowly avoiding the cat, Annie said, "Sorry to interrupt, but do you have a second?"

"Hi." Sam glanced up. "Tweety Bird and I are glad to see you."

Tweety Bird must be the goshawk, his cartoon name courtesy of Lyndsey.

"It's about my mother."

"Sure. Give me a second." He resumed instructing Gus, pointing out where to place the nail. "That's it, buddy."

Gus struggled, the hammer too heavy for his small hands. Succeeding at last, he grinned broadly.

Sam rubbed the boy's buzz cut. "We'll make a carpenter out of you yet."

Gus gazed up at Sam as if he were king of the world.

Annie could relate. She'd recently stared at Sam with similar adoration.

"What's up?" He left the kids to their own devices and joined her.

Not wanting them to hear, she motioned him a few feet away. "You hired my mother."

His smile dimmed marginally, but the twinkle in his eyes remained. "Guilty as charged."

"Why?"

"I had an opening for a guest-relations manager. She has the experience."

"What about the inn? This morning I retained your architect and spoke to your contractor. We're moving ahead. The architect is starting on the drawings and the contractor's putting together a quote to clear the land."

"Annie, the same goes for your mother and Irma and Lester. They're free to leave as soon as the inn is up and running."

"Lester?" She blinked at him in disbelief. "You hired our maintenance man, too?"

"Didn't I tell you?"

"He's working for Valley Community Church."

"The job was temporary. They let him go last week."

"What! I—I didn't know."

"Being unemployed isn't something a man like Lester brags about."

What was left of Annie's anger deflated, like a sail without wind. Lester was a man of few means but an abundance of pride. Despite a mild mental disability, the result of a fall down an abandoned well as a child, he'd always supported himself. He was good, kind, sweet and loved by all. He was also a decent handyman and had worked for the Hennessys the past twelve years.

Of everyone who'd lost their job when the inn had burned, Annie felt the worst for Lester. Irma at least had her husband, and the others were only part-time or seasonal. Lester was alone.

"I'm glad you hired him. He needs to be working."

"So does your mother."

Sam was right. "I just wish you'd called me first."

"I assumed she'd discussed the job with you."

"This isn't only about her. I depend on her to watch Nessa while I'm at work. If she's going to be bringing Nessa here every day, I have a right to be part of that decision."

"You do. It was thoughtless of me to exclude you."

Annie exhaled slowly, not completely trusting his sincerity. "Sometimes it seems like you're...undermining me."

"That's not my intention. I swear. I'm just being a friend."

"By offering my mother a job."

"I figured it would motivate Gary to lay off you."

"I'm not sure he'll be any happier with Nessa being underfoot here all day, passed off from one person to the next. I'm not sure I'm happy."

"It's short-term," he reminded her.

She should be relieved. Her mother having a job was a godsend. They'd have extra money to put toward new furnishings for the inn and a larger place to live, if one became available. Her mother would have purpose again, a reason to get out of bed in the mornings and face the day with anticipation rather than despair.

All because of Sam.

Except he'd gone behind her back. Probably because he suspected she'd object. Unless, as he claimed, he was being a friend to her and her entire family.

Was she so focused on herself and the inn that she dismissed the equally important needs of her loved ones? And her mother working did put them one step closer to their goal of rebuilding the inn.

"I'd better go, let Mom know everything's okay. She's worried."

"*Is* everything okay?"

She recalled the last time he'd looked at her with such uncertainty. He'd been twenty-two and leaving for the job in California. In between goodbye kisses, he promised he'd return soon and asked her to wait for him. She'd been twenty-four, deeply in love, desperate to get married and trying her best to put up a brave front.

In one short year, their love unraveled.

Annie had laid the blame on Sam. A bad marriage taught her much of the blame lay with her. Two people were necessary to make a relationship and two to break it.

"Yeah, it's okay," she assured him. "The job's a good fit for Mom. And Nessa will be here only on the days Gary doesn't have her. Next time, however—" she leveled a finger at him "—call me first."

"You got it." Sam grinned. "Before you go, take a look at Tweety Bird."

Annie owed him that much for taking in the hawk.

They went over to the chicken coop. If Tweety Bird was grateful she'd rescued him, he didn't show it and glared at her menacingly.

"Dr. Murry examined him yesterday," Sam said after warning the kids to stay out of the toolbox. "He thinks most of the injuries are superficial."

"Did he have an opinion about what happened?"

"Same as you. Attacked by a larger flying predator."

"Has he taken any food and water yet?" Annie asked.

"Raw sirloin's his favorite. Though he likes chicken, too. I assume he's drinking, though I haven't seen him do it. He keeps to his roost whenever anyone's around. Dr. Murry estimates a week, maybe two, and we can release him. I'm thinking of Grey Rock Point. The fire bypassed most of that area."

"I'd like to be there, if I can."

"Wouldn't think of releasing him without you." Sam glanced over his shoulder at the kids, then at Annie. "I owe you."

"For what?" It seemed to Annie quite the opposite was true.

"Your advice about Lyndsey. She's been lost since Trisha died. The animals, well, they've made a difference. A big one. She's becoming more like her old self every day."

"You did that entirely on your own, Sam."

"Spending the summer in Sweetheart has been good for both of us."

"How long until you leave?" She expected him to say in the next couple weeks, given that school started soon.

"I'm not sure." He shrugged one shoulder. "We may stay awhile longer."

"Stay? Are you serious?"

"Why not? I always figured on going back and forth. Lately, I've been thinking of more forth and less back."

"What about the ranch in California?"

"According to my father-in-law, the foreman's pulling his weight." Sam chuckled. "For all I know, he's after my job."

"And you're not worried?"

"I should be. I stole the last foreman's job." They both sobered at the reminder of nine years ago.

"Doesn't Lyndsey start school soon?"

"I could send her home. She'd probably hate that. For someone who completely resisted coming here, she really likes it. Gus may have something to do with that. I keep reminding myself they're too young for me to worry. They are too young, aren't they?"

The question was directed more to himself than Annie.

"Wouldn't you miss her if you sent her home?"

"Yeah. A lot. Better I enroll her in school here."

"Is the construction not going well?" A delay could be the reason for his sudden change of plans.

"It's going great. We'll be ready for our first guests next week."

"That soon!"

"Well, we have to get some reservations first. Our secretary at the ranch in California hired a website designer and is researching the best places to advertise. Mayor Dempsey also made some suggestions. She thinks we should have a grand-opening weekend. I told her we'd have to wait for the shipment of calves to arrive. The truck's due Monday, and we haven't even started construction on the livestock holding pens."

The mayor was giving Sam suggestions to promote his business? That shouldn't be a surprise. If successful, the Gold Nugget would be a boon to Sweetheart.

"Sounds like everything's coming together."

"Annie." Sam squeezed her arm. "What's really bothering you?"

"Nothing."

"You act like you don't want me to stay."

In truth, she did and she didn't. Sam had the ability to create as much chaos for her as calm. "I'm honestly not sure how I feel."

He moved closer. "Aren't you?"

"There's nothing between us, if that's what you're implying."

"You were never a good liar."

"Just because we shared a couple kisses—"

"Exactly because we shared a couple of kisses."

She shook her head and retreated a step. "We're not the same people we once were. Things have changed."

"I get that you haven't completely forgiven me for leaving you."

"I'm not holding a grudge," she insisted. *Not a big one.*

"You did start seeing Gary before we officially broke up."

The mild accusation annoyed her. "We went to lunch."

"Twice."

She resisted asking him who'd tattled on her. It didn't matter. "I hadn't heard from you in six weeks."

"So you executed plan B."

"It wasn't like that." Only it had been like that. Annie was terrified Sam had dumped her and that she'd wind up the next Hennessy old maid.

Perhaps she was still terrified and that was what held her back. He hadn't cut all his ties to California and could leave again.

"I was working my tail off, trying to get ahead. Saving up enough money for a ring."

"A ring?" The bones in her legs went weak. "Why didn't you tell me?"

"I was going to surprise you with it. Then I heard about Gary. And you were acting distant."

"I was hurt."

"So hurt you married him?"

"After you left. Almost a year after you left." She couldn't help sounding defensive.

"And I got married a mere four months later."

"To a woman who was pregnant with your baby." That was what hurt the most.

"I didn't cheat on you, Annie. I swear. We'd already split up when Trisha and I started dating."

"Barely just split up. You moved on at lightning speed."

"Why did you care? You were already seeing Gary."

"I wasn't seeing him. Not romantically."

"No, you just had him waiting in the wings."

"You make me sound awful when you're the one who deserted me."

"To take a better job. Isn't that what the man's supposed to do? Provide for his wife."

"I didn't need you to provide for me."

"No, you could provide for yourself just fine, thanks to your family's business. I'm the one who needed to make my mark."

Her deepest, darkest fear tumbled out. "I thought you were running away. That you didn't love me anymore."

"I thought the same thing when I heard about Gary."

The revelations, rather than bring them together, hung in the air like a poisonous cloud.

"Hey, Daddy." Lyndsey and Gus scampered over. "We're going to feed the kits and the goats."

Annie swallowed her reply to Sam. She wouldn't argue in front of the kids. She wouldn't argue any more with Sam, either.

"Thanks again for giving Mom a job," she said stiffly. "I'll see you later."

"I'd like to continue this conversation."

Another man wanting to "continue the conversation." She'd had her fill of them. "What would that accomplish other than reopening old wounds?"

She had just started toward the house when a car pulled into the driveway. Annie didn't recognize it, but then there were a lot of vehicles coming and going at the ranch.

The man waited at the walkway for her, and then asked, "Ms. Hennessy?"

"Yes?"

Her heart momentarily stalled. Had Gary made good on his threat about revisiting their child custody agreement? Was this a process server? He was carrying a manila envelope. Why had she answered yes when he asked her name?

"Good to meet you." The man extended his hand. "I'm Dermitt Wilson."

The architect!

Relief flooded her. "Nice to meet you." She gripped his hand. Possibly too hard. "What are you doing here?"

"A last-minute meeting with Sam. I was hoping to find you and kill two birds with one stone." He handed her the manila envelope. "That contains preliminary artist renderings of the inn. I thought you might want a look before I finalize them and start drawing the plans."

Artist renderings. The architect's vision of the new inn, based on her description.

"Already?"

"I worked all morning. Your story inspired me."

Excitement coursed through Annie as she opened the envelope and drew out the heavy sheets of paper.

She couldn't believe her eyes. This wasn't the Sweetheart Inn. It was even more beautiful.

"WHAT DO YOU THINK?"

Sam studied the cabin floor plan the architect had given him. The design was simple and functional, yet attractive. He could easily envision his guests staying there and being comfortable.

"I like it."

"Good. See anything that needs changing?"

He pointed to the bathroom. "This looks a little small."

"I can enlarge it, but I'll have to reduce the size of the closet."

"Do it. Most women I know would appreciate a larger bathroom. And the closets only need to hold a week's worth of clothes."

Sam and Dermitt Wilson stood in an empty field at the Gold Nugget, each holding one end of the plans for the guest cabins. Dermitt, who usually wore nice slacks and a button-down shirt, had chosen jeans and athletic shoes for his second visit to the ranch in three days.

"How many cabins did you say you're going to build?" he asked.

"Six to start with." Sam had already hired the surveyor and the engineer. They were scheduled to begin work tomorrow. "Six more next spring if things take off."

"Do those six include your personal one?"

"No." Sam flipped to the next sheet, on which were the electrical and plumbing specifications for the guest cabins. He didn't pretend to understand them. "I still need to decide where to build."

"The hill over there is a good possibility."

Sam's gaze followed Dermitt's. The hill was separate from the guest cabins but not too far. Perfect for the three-bedroom deluxe cabin he was planning for him and Lyndsey.

Or should he change it to four bedrooms? Just in case.

In case Annie changed her mind about there being anything between them? According to their heated exchange earlier in the week, that was pretty unlikely. Especially when they hadn't spoken since then.

Better to stick with three bedrooms. For now.

The rumbling of a truck and stock trailer had Sam and the architect looking away from the hill and toward the ranch house. Will was walking out from the barn to greet the oversize rig.

"Appears my calves are arriving ahead of schedule," Sam said.

Fortunately they'd recently finished constructing the livestock holding pens.

Dermitt rolled up the plans into a tube and secured them with a rubber band. "I'll revise these to include a bigger bathroom and drop off a new set on Monday."

"Hate for you to make another trip up here just to deliver plans."

"No problem. I'll already be here. I have a meeting with Annie Hennessy to review the preliminary drawings for the inn."

He'd told Sam the other day how much Annie had liked his initial rendering, a smaller and more affordable version of the original inn.

The two men strode across the empty field, Sam in a hurry and Dermitt keeping up. At the house, they parted. Sam caught up with Will at the livestock pens. The driver was backing up to the gate Will held open.

"Need any help?" Sam asked over the loud chorus of bawling calves and idling diesel engine.

"You're welcome to watch."

If Will was half as good with calves as horses, all Sam would be doing was watching.

With the ramp lowered, the calves, eighteen in all, spilled from the trailer in a small stampede. They were a variety of longhorns and jerseys, their coats ranging from black to red to light brown. Finding the water trough, the calves immediately slaked their thirst and then investigated the feeders.

Will shut the gate behind the last one while Sam signed the bill of lading the driver presented him. The truck and empty trailer no sooner pulled forward than Sam and Will rested their forearms and boot soles on the pen railing and studied Sam's latest purchase.

"You order the dewormer and vaccinations yet?" Will asked.

"They're in the supply room."

"Tan one looks kind of puny."

Sam agreed. "Maybe we should put him by himself for a while. Till he grows some."

Will merely nodded.

"You set a time with that buddy of yours yet?"

They discussed Will's acquaintance with the used roping

equipment for sale until Sam's cell phone rang. His pulse spiked at the name and number on the display screen.

"Hey, Annie. How's it go—"

"Sam, sorry to bother you." She sounded rushed and anxious.

"No problem. What's up?"

"I'm trying to find my mother. Is she there?"

"She went to the warehouse store in Reno for supplies."

"Shoot. She must be out of range. Every time I call it goes straight to voice mail."

"Is something wrong?"

"No. Yes, but I'll take care of it."

"Are you sure?"

"I am." After a pause, she blurted, "Actually, I'm not sure. I hate to impose."

"Tell me."

"Wanda DeMarco called me. She's one of the grade-school teachers. Granny's at the inn. I have no idea how she got there. Wanda tried to give her a ride home, but Granny refused and became agitated when Wanda started insisting. She actually ordered Wanda off the place. I'm worried. It's not safe for Granny there alone."

Sam didn't hesitate. "I'll leave right now."

"Are you sure? I can be there in an hour. If you could just check on her…"

"I'll call you from the inn."

"It seems I'm always thanking you," Annie admitted.

"I'm here anytime you need me."

They disconnected. Will waved Sam away when he started to explain the situation.

"I've got this covered, boss."

"See you later." Sam had no doubts the puny calf would be moved to a different pen and the entire herd dewormed and vaccinated by the time he got home.

Irma assured him she'd watch Lyndsey. Not that he could have pried his daughter away from Gus.

Fifteen minutes later Sam arrived at the inn and parked. He'd witnessed the ruins up close before, but the devastation rocked him anew. This wasn't some random home or building. It was a place where he'd spent endless hours for two years of his life with people he cared about.

Some of those hours in Annie's bed, making sweet love to her.

It was also a place that might have been spared had he disobeyed orders the day of the fire.

"Granny Orla," he called out, the heavy weight pressing on the inside of his chest making it difficult to breathe. Reaching the entrance to the inn, he called her name again.

Had she left between the time Annie phoned him and he arrived?

"In here," came a faint response.

He found Granny in what was once a sitting room off the lobby, on her hands and knees, digging through rubble.

"Be careful. You'll hurt yourself."

"I'm fine. Don't you worry." She was filthy from head to toes.

"Let me help you." He knelt beside her. "What are you looking for?"

"My book. It used to be on a shelf in this room."

All that remained was one exterior wall, the entire surface scorched black, and the floor, three feet deep in places with debris.

"I don't think it's here, Granny." He laid a gentle hand on her shoulder.

She sat back on her calves, the movement stiff as if her joints ached—or her heart had become too weighted with grief for her small body to carry.

"I'm not crazy."

"I know that."

"You look at me like Annie does. The same worry on your face."

"We care about you." Sam's voice had grown thick. He was responsible for this, too. Granny Orla had always been sharp as a tack.

"It's easier sometimes," she said softly, "not to face the real world. Sort of a mental vacation."

"I understand."

"I imagine you do." She looked at him directly without a trace of confusion. "Must have been hard losing your wife. A lot of guilt. A lot of regrets."

"More than you can imagine." Sam suffered a fresh wave of both.

"I always felt terrible about you and Annie. You both went off and married the first person you stumbled across."

Stumbled across. An interesting way to describe the start of his and Trisha's relationship. She'd certainly put herself in Sam's path, the second he'd returned to California after breaking up with Annie.

"I don't regret my marriage."

"Course you don't. You'd be a fool if you did. That's a beautiful little girl you have."

"As is your great-granddaughter."

"She's a dickens, all right. I think she takes after me."

"No doubt about it. A Hennessy through and through."

"I hope she's smarter than the rest of us." Granny Orla rolled something around in her hand.

Until the movement caught Sam's eye, he hadn't noticed. "You're all pretty smart as far as I'm concerned."

"Not when it comes to men. You've heard the rumors. Probably scared you silly when you were younger."

"I did want to marry Annie."

"Eventually. But you weren't ready, and she was in an all-fired hurry. Makes for a bad combination." Granny sighed. "She was bound and determined to escape the Hennessy curse. Problem was, she didn't have the whole story. Her father no more abandoned Fiona than her grandfather abandoned me."

"What happened?"

"We refused to go with them. They wanted us with a powerful passion, make no mistake. And us them. But we couldn't leave Sweetheart. It was the same with Annie when you asked her to go with you to California."

"I did more than ask."

"She couldn't tear herself away. Not her fault. She inherited that same awful stubborn streak from me that her mother did."

"The thing is, we could have returned in a couple of years, once I'd saved up some money and gotten ahead in my job."

"She was impatient. And worried."

"That you and Fiona couldn't run the inn by yourselves?"

"Heavens, no." Granny Orla's smile was that of a young woman. "That she loved you more than the inn."

"I doubt that." His stomach tightened. "There isn't much Annie puts ahead of the inn."

Granny opened her hand, revealing a tiny blackened jewelry case. One corner had been rubbed clean, revealing the silver finish underneath.

In spite of its ravaged condition, Sam immediately recognized the case, and his chest constricted. It had once contained a heart-shaped pendant with an opal mounted in the center. He'd given the necklace to Annie for her twentieth-fourth birthday. Less than three months before he'd left.

"She kept this on her dresser always," Granny said, placing the case in Sam's hands. "Even after she married Gary. Don't think she told him where it and the pendant came from, but I'm sure he suspected."

"I can't take this. It belongs to Annie."

"I thought maybe you'd want to give it to her. She's accumulating quite a collection of things from the inn."

Sam balanced the case in his palm and carefully opened the lid. It was empty, the velvet lining having been incinerated.

"The necklace was lost in the fire," he said. Emotions, raw and powerful, overtook him. He cleared his throat.

"Oh, it wasn't lost." Granny Orla's eyes lit up. "Annie has it. One of the first things she grabbed when we got the notice to evacuate."

Sam closed the lid on the case and folded his fingers protectively around it. Annie still had the necklace he'd given her.

No way could he leave Sweetheart now.

Chapter Twelve

Annie raced back to town the instant she could cut loose from work, dreading what she might find. Her grandmother was at the ruins of the inn again. With Fiona working, no one was home to watch Granny Orla or hear the new door alarm screeching.

Was Annie's life ever going to return to normal?

Not for a while, but tiny pinpoints of light had recently appeared at the end of the tunnel.

Gary hadn't backed down completely about revisiting their custody agreement. He had agreed, however, to give Annie a little more time when she told him about her mother's new job and being on the wait list for a three-bedroom house to rent—one with a small backyard for Nessa. If all went well, they could move the following month.

Though her mother still had her moments—didn't they all?—she was much improved and left for work with a spring in her step. Annie had every faith that when construction started on the inn, Fiona would be her old self.

There were also the drawings for the inn, which the architect had promised would be done later this week. She couldn't wait. At least ten times a day Annie pulled out the renderings.

It was their old inn, but different. More functional with a nod to the modern while still maintaining the country charm of the original. Less square footage but designed for easy future additions. Most important, it could be built within their budget if they held off on replacing some of the original antiques.

She and her mother had settled with the insurance company earlier that week and were expecting a check in the mail any day. Annie was relieved. Signing the agreement had worked a sort of magic, allowing her to move forward emotionally.

She had to acknowledge Sam's part in her turnaround. Without a doubt the architect's *very reasonable* retainer and the construction contractor's *enormously fair* bid to clear the land were his doing. He'd done so much for her already, including rescuing her grandmother today.

Annie hated admitting it, but for once she was glad Gary had Nessa for the day. At least Annie didn't have to worry about her daughter as well as her grandmother.

She would have to do something about Granny Orla and soon, Annie just didn't know what. There were no doctors in Sweetheart specializing in geriatric medicine. No professional grief counselors or organized support groups. Only so much assistance available on the internet.

Several victims of the fire did meet regularly to talk and share and give each other strength. Annie had tried once to coerce her mother and grandmother into attending a meeting with her. The attempt was met with resistance. Maybe she should try again.

Several pieces of the yellow caution tape surrounding the inn had come loose from the metal posts and were fluttering in the summer breeze like party streamers. Annie didn't concern herself with refastening them. The construction contractor would remove the tape and posts in order to erect temporary fencing around the property.

Granny Orla and Sam were standing beside his truck, chatting amiably, when she pulled into the lot beside them. All that concern for nothing, Annie thought. Her grandmother looked fine.

Sam looked…mouthwatering. There were no other words. His jeans hugged his lean hips, his short-sleeved Western shirt stretched taut across his broad shoulders, his Stetson was pulled forward at a rakish angle.

Without thinking, she reached a hand up to the opening of her uniform shirt and felt for the necklace he'd given her. Lately, she'd been wearing it more often. If only she'd remembered to grab the silver jewelry case the necklace had come in during the evacuation.

"Granny," she scolded the second she got out of the SUV. "You can't just leave the apartment without telling anyone. And how in the world did you get here?"

"I walked." Granny's small chest puffed out. "And you're not the boss of me, young lady."

Not the boss of her? Where had her grandmother picked up that phrase?

"If you wanted to come here, you should have waited until I got off work."

"Like you'd have brought me."

Probably true.

"Why didn't you let Wanda give you a ride home?"

"Her car's always a mess."

Annie resisted expelling a tired sigh. "That's no reason."

"If I let Wanda give me a ride home, then this handsome man wouldn't have shown up to keep me company." Granny slipped her arm through Sam's.

Annie didn't know whether to laugh or cry. She turned to Sam. "You have an admirer."

"It goes both ways. We had a real nice talk before you got here."

"Oh?" Annie didn't like the sound of that and strove for nonchalance. "What did you two talk about?"

"Your collection of things salvaged from the fire."

Whew! That wasn't such a dangerous topic. "I saw Wanda the other day. She told me people have been storing some of their more valuable recovered possessions in the basement at the chapel next door. Especially those with historic significance. Apparently, there's quite an assortment."

"I'd like to see what's there. I bet a lot of people would." Sam sought her gaze and held it. "I'd like to see what you have."

"Nothing much." She laughed—a little too nervously. "A candlestick, a key, a padlock. I wish I could find more. They'll start clearing the lot soon. When the soil tests are complete." She forced herself to look at the ruins. "I should probably come back on my day off and go through this mess one last time."

"I'll help you."

"Me, too," Granny Orla added. "And Fiona. We'll make it a family outing."

Annie noticed that *Sam* noticed Granny had included him as part of the family. Was her grandmother having another episode?

She didn't think so. Granny had always adored Sam and had probably hoped he'd be her grandson-in-law one day.

He held out his hand toward Annie. "In the meantime, you can add this to your collection."

She stared at the jewelry case, everything inside her going still. "When did you find that?"

"Granny Orla did. Today."

"I can't believe it. I thought I'd lost this forever."

"Maybe there's a reason Granny found it when she did." He waited for her to take the case.

She did, cupping it in her palms. "Thank you." The case felt warm. Sam's heat, she realized. Now seeping into her.

Tears filled her eyes as another piece of her former life was returned to her.

"Amazing something that small and delicate could come

through the fire intact," he said. "Well, almost intact. The velvet lining was burned away. But there was bound to be some damage."

"I suppose." She traced the intricate scroll pattern on the lid with her fingertip as she'd done countless times, always thinking of Sam when she did.

He watched her. "With some cleaning and a little repair, it'll be as good as new."

He was likening them and their relationship to the jewelry case. Did that mean he thought they had survived their painful pasts, superficially damaged but intact underneath, enough to forge a new relationship?

Even if she did want a relationship with Sam, it wasn't what she needed. Not until the new inn was built and they'd moved to the new house. Her family and their welfare had to come first.

"I don't know about the good-as-new part," she said. "It's going to take a lot of cleaning and polishing."

"I'm good at cleaning and polishing."

Resisting the pull of his blue eyes was impossible. Against her will, she was drawn into their depths.

He had her, and his half smile told her he was well aware of it, too. If she could, she'd grab hold of her shirtfront and shake some sense into herself. Instead, she murmured, "We'll see."

"I'll buy the silver cleaner."

"I have some already."

"Then we're good to go."

Shivers traveled up her spine.

This couldn't be happening. She blinked in an effort to clear her head. Sam wasn't going to divert her from her plans. Not again.

"Wonderful idea!" Granny Orla beamed. "Come to breakfast on Saturday. After you finish cleaning the jewelry case, we'll all come here."

"I accept," Sam said before Annie could protest, his smile widening.

She could put up a fight but chose not to. It was only breakfast after all. And cleaning the jewelry case.

"We can look for my book."

The spell Sam had cast promptly broke and reality returned. "Granny, I don't think your book is here."

"Won't know for sure unless we scour the place."

"All right," she relented. "Saturday it is."

Granny preened with satisfaction.

Humoring her, Annie asked, "What's so important about this book anyway?"

"How else can I remember what the inn was like before the fire?"

"We'll never forget the inn." She squeezed her grandmother's shoulders.

"None of us will," Sam agreed.

"My memory's not what it used to be. Having something tangible to hold on to will make remembering easier. The new inn won't be the same."

"True. But it'll be nice." Annie had shown her family the artist rendering. She assumed Granny had loved it, too.

"Won't be the same," she repeated to herself, and straightened her spine. "Which is why I've decided to retire."

Granny Orla's announcement wasn't entirely a surprise. She'd frequently kidded about retiring. This time, however, she spoke with a ring of conviction that left no doubt. Annie's hopes of running the newly rebuilt Sweetheart Inn with all three Hennessy women working side by side were soundly dashed.

SAM NUDGED THE large buckskin into a lope, and they circled the makeshift arena at an easy pace. The horse, Will had called him Cholula, responded well to Sam's commands. Obedient and strong, but with a touch of spirit and a mind of his own. Exactly the kind of horse Sam liked to ride.

Reining Cholula to a stop at the fence where Will stood, he said, "Tell your buddy I'll take him."

"Already did."

"You were that sure?"

As always, Will's casual shrug spoke volumes. He had Sam pegged and had matched him with a horse he was confident Sam would like.

"Did you also negotiate the price on my behalf?"

"Talked him down as far as he'll go."

Sam nodded approvingly at the amount Will cited. "Let's keep him in the barn until the new stalls are finished next week."

"Luiz is already laying down fresh sawdust."

Will was quickly becoming indispensable. Good thing. Sam needed reliable staff to cover for him during his visits to California.

His father-in-law had taken the news of Sam's decision to make Sweetheart his home base better than expected. He'd made only two requests during their hour-long phone conversation the previous night: that Sam allow Lyndsey lengthy visits during summer vacations and holidays and that he return home for a few weeks to wrap up any loose ends and walk the new foreman through preparations for the fall cattle roundup.

It wasn't too much to ask, and Sam readily agreed. His one problem was what to do about Lyndsey and school, which started soon. He'd debated his options long into the night when he should have been sleeping.

Lyndsey would have to come home with him, there was no other choice. Her grandfather would want to see her and she him. But a few weeks was a lot of school to miss.

If she returned to Sweetheart early, who would she stay with? Irma had enough of her own children to worry about.

Annie didn't have the room. Sam wasn't comfortable leaving Lyndsey with anyone else.

He didn't want to think about the raccoon kits. They'd have to be surrendered to the wildlife refuge before he and Lyndsey left, and she'd be heartsick.

He decided to call his father-in-law back tonight. If they could arrange for a tutor in California and homeschool Lyndsey during their visit, she could resume public school here in Sweetheart when they returned and not have to work so hard catching up.

With one problem potentially settled, Sam dismounted, his test drive with Cholula at a satisfactory end.

"Have you ridden the west ridge yet?" he asked Will on their walk to the barn.

"Yesterday afternoon."

"And?"

"First mile's clear."

"But the next ten miles aren't."

Will's nod confirmed Sam had come to the correct conclusion.

"How long to get the job done?"

"A week. With enough men and the right equipment."

An expensive undertaking. Also a necessary one if Sam wanted safe and navigable trails for his guests to ride.

"What about the terrain?"

Will became even more quiet than usual. "Folks won't be raving about the view anymore."

Not about its beauty, anyway. "Is the north side any better?"

"I'll ride out there tomorrow."

They continued their discussion inside the barn while Sam unsaddled Cholula and settled him in the stall next to the pony. The big gelding made himself right at home, apparently liking Sam and their future prospects together as much as Sam did.

On their way to the cattle pens, Sam's and Will's attention was drawn to an official-looking SUV pulling onto the ranch. Sam caught the county sheriff's logo on the driver's side door just as it opened and a uniformed man stepped out. Mayor Dempsey accompanied him.

Sam grinned as he strode forward to meet the law-enforcement official. "I thought the citizens in these parts were smarter than to elect you sheriff."

"I'm surprised you had the nerve to show your face here after all these years," Cliff Dempsey answered, just as good-naturedly.

They shook hands, Sam noting the strength in the other man's grip. He and Cliff had been acquaintances when he lived here before. Cliff had worked part-time at the Paydirt for his aunt while Sam had been a ranch hand. Then, Sam had left for California and Cliff enrolled in the Vegas Police Academy.

Sam hadn't seen Cliff since his arrival in Sweetheart. When he asked, he'd been told Cliff was in Ohio, helping his cousin and her children return home after a messy divorce.

Apparently, he was back on the job, for he produced his citation book from his back pocket.

"Did I commit a violation?" Sam asked as Cliff produced his citation book from his back pocket.

"Not you. Your construction contractor. Is he here?"

"At the corrals. We're building new stalls. Can I ask what he's done?"

"Illegally parked his trucks in town."

"Hmm. Don't suppose you could cut him some slack. It's for a good cause."

"I have. Up till now. But Miranda Staley's sworn if I don't do something, she'll file a complaint against me. And given that the election's next year…"

"I get it. Do your job." Sam decided not to argue, and simply reimburse the contractor the cost of the ticket. Also warn him to avoid parking in front of Miranda Staley's house.

"Can't really blame her," the mayor added. "She has five residents in her elder-care group home. Getting them in and out and around is challenging enough without having to navigate fully loaded construction vehicles."

The mayor waited with Sam while Cliff sought out the construction contractor and performed his duty.

"This place looks fantastic." Her smile reflected the admiration in her voice. "How soon until you open?"

"I was going to stop by the Paydirt on my next trip to town and deliver the good news. We've got our first reservations. Three, actually."

"Oh, my God! That's wonderful." She threw herself at Sam, surprising him and nearly knocking him off his feet. "When do they arrive? And are they getting married?"

"'Fraid not." He peeled her gently away. "The first guests will be here mid-August."

"That's less than two weeks away!"

"They understand we're still remodeling, but they don't care. They're husband and wife wildlife photographers. On assignment to take pictures of the animals and their habitats post-fire for some nature magazine. The other two reservations are for families. Their kids want to learn team roping."

"We don't have much time."

"For what?"

"A grand opening."

"The ranch? I'm not sure—"

"The whole town." She gestured wildly. "We'll call it a reopening."

"Mayor Dempsey, with all due respect, I don't think three reservations are enough to warrant a grand opening."

Her features fell, then immediately lifted. "But you'll have more. This is only the beginning."

"The beginning of what?" Annie asked.

Sam had been so preoccupied, he'd missed her arrival, not that he was expecting her. She must have parked at the house and stopped to check on her mother and daughter first. Whatever the reason, he was always glad to see her.

He'd spent half the day with her on Saturday at the inn ruins. Fiona and Granny Orla, too. It might have been the company. Or the difficult and emotional task of sifting through a ton of debris with very little to show for it. Possibly Granny's nonstop talk of retirement. But there had been no special moments between him and Annie. Not like when he'd given her the jewelry case.

"We have our first reservations," he said, studying her face and gauging her reaction.

She didn't reveal much. "That's great. Congratulations."

"I was saying to Sam," Mayor Dempsey injected, "that we should have a grand reopening. For the entire town. We can promote the event, use it to entice even more tourists." She gasped excitedly, her hand flying to her chest. "I know, we could run a contest. The first couple to marry in Sweetheart after the fire can have a free week's stay at the Gold Nugget."

"Seems a little premature," Annie said.

Sam didn't think he'd ever witnessed a flatter smile. "I agree. We only have three rooms available."

"But there's the RV Resort," the mayor continued. "That place was hardly touched in the fire. Well, except for two of the cabins. They're gone. But four cabins are left and all those RV parking spots. And the Mountainside Motel. They have twenty rooms."

"I'm sure it'll be very successful."

Mayor Dempsey was too caught up in her idea to notice Annie's forced enthusiasm.

Not Sam. His goal was always to help the town and bring back the tourists. He just hated that they wouldn't be staying at the Sweetheart Inn. Annie must hate it, too.

Cliff returned, his citation book stuffed in his back pocket.

His aunt immediately launched into the news about Sam's reservations and the town's grand reopening.

"I'm going to take a peek at the kits," Annie told Sam, excusing herself. "Is Lyndsey in the barn?"

"She's with the kits or the goats or the hawk. Just look for Gus. Wherever he is, you'll find Lyndsey."

After Annie left, he escorted Cliff and his aunt to their vehicle. The two men made plans to meet up for a beer before Sam's trip to California. He had just seen the mayor and sheriff off when the contractor strolled over from the horse stalls, waving the citation.

"I'll take care of that," Sam assured him.

"No worries. My fault. We're working on the house next door to Ms. Staley. I should have verified with her before blocking her driveway."

Sam liked the construction contractor. A few years older than Sam, Chas had an easygoing demeanor that was the complete opposite of his nose-to-the-grindstone work ethic.

"Is there a problem?" Sam asked.

"I noticed Annie Hennessy arrived. We have a meeting."

That explained her unannounced appearance. "She's in the barn with my daughter."

They found Annie by the kits' cage. Alone. Lyndsey and Gus must be elsewhere.

She was sitting on the floor, Porky cradled to her chest, and furiously wiping at her eyes with the hem of her shirt.

Sam felt the blow like a kick to his stomach. He'd hoped he was through with making Annie cry.

Chapter Thirteen

"You're here." Annie returned Porky to the cage and stood, greeting Sam and the construction contractor. "That didn't take long. The mayor must have been in a hurry."

"You know how she gets." Sam's tone was apologetic.

"I didn't see Lyndsey or Gus." She hadn't looked, either. Glad to find the barn empty, she'd let the unexpected tears fall.

The Gold Nugget Ranch was hosting its first guests. A dream that had once been hers. Now, it belonged to Sam.

She was glad for him. Glad for the town. Mayor Dempsey was right in suggesting there be a celebration.

Annie was also jealous. Her envy reached every fiber of her being. The Sweetheart Inn should be the reason people flocked to town.

Adding salt to the wound, the ranch was where her mother was now employed, along with the Hennessys' former housekeeper and maintenance man. The place where her daughter spent many a day under her grandmother's care while Annie was at work.

More and more, her life was revolving around the Gold Nugget. She should be grateful, and she was. That didn't lessen her anguish, however.

"Nice to see you again, Chas." She mustered a smile for

the contractor, hoping he hadn't noticed anything amiss when he came into the barn.

"A pleasure, Annie."

She avoided looking at Sam. His concerned expression would break down her hard-won resolve.

"I was wondering, could Chas and I use your kitchen table to go over the drawings? The one at the apartment is too tiny."

"Of course." Sam nodded to both Annie and Chas. "I'll leave you to your business. The back door to the house is open."

"Would you…" Annie decided she was certifiably crazy but asked anyway. "Would you mind joining us?"

His brows rose. "You sure?"

"I could use another opinion, and you have far more experience when it comes to construction than me."

"I wouldn't say that, but I'd be happy to sit in."

Fiona, Irma and all the kids, including Lyndsey and Gus, made themselves scarce, cleaning or playing in other rooms. Chas unrolled the drawings and laid them out on the large oak kitchen table while Sam and Annie took seats across from each other.

Her mood instantly improved. In fact, it soared. "Wow!"

The floor plans were on top: basement, ground floor and second story. She loved, loved, loved the design. Spacious, yet efficient. Chas pointed out the areas where even more money could be saved. Replacing some of those antiques might actually be possible.

"It's perfect," she exclaimed when Chas was done explaining the supplemental pages.

"I glad you like it." He grinned at her praise.

"What's our next step?"

"Keep the drawings. Go over them for a few days or a week. Something may occur to you, a change you want to make. In the meantime, we clear the lot."

"How soon can we start?"

"As soon as the soil tests are completed. Here's a proposal from the engineering company."

Annie glanced at the document. "What will the tests show?" She wondered how different residential testing was from the ones she'd been running in the field over the last several weeks.

"General condition of the soil. Rate of erosion. How stable it is. How much contamination."

"Contamination?"

"The inn was old, constructed long before modern building codes were in place. There could have been lead-based paint and treated wood. Any number of things. When a house or building burns, those toxins seep into the soil."

"And if the soil's contaminated?"

"We treat it."

"What does that involve?"

He made the process of removing the soil, treating it and then replacing it once it was decontaminated sound simple.

Annie suspected the opposite was true and remained skeptical. "That sounds expensive."

"I won't lie, Annie. It isn't cheap."

"How much?" She braced herself. What had started out so well was going rapidly downhill.

Sam reached across the table and put a hand on her arm. "You've come this far. You can't rebuild without clearing the land, and you can't do that without having the tests. Might as well get them over with."

"Just so you know," Chas said, "the tests we've done on other properties in town have shown normal or low levels of toxicity. Unless your inn was constructed with vastly different materials, it should have the same results."

Both men sat watching her, waiting for her to decide. She clicked the pen over and over.

Sam was right. If she didn't consent to the tests, the inn would definitely never be rebuilt.

"Where do I sign?"

Chas pointed to the engineer's proposal. Her fingers trembled only briefly before she scrawled her signature across the bottom line.

"Here you go."

He placed the proposal inside his portfolio. "We'll get started right away."

"Thank you." Annie felt fresh tears prick her eyes. These ones were of joy. She'd taken another step to regaining her old life and finding her happily-ever-after.

She escorted Chas to the back door. Sam was about to leave with him—Chas had asked him to inspect the foundations for the new guest cabins that had been poured earlier—but Annie stopped him.

"Do you have a minute?"

"Sure."

Sam had always been the impetuous one, though Annie was eager to follow his lead and usually glad she did.

Today, she took the initiative.

The moment the door was closed behind Chas, she reached for Sam and pulled his head down to meet her hungry lips.

His stupor didn't last. Within seconds, he had her pinned against the door.

"What was that for?" he asked when they paused long enough to catch their breath.

She arched into him. "Does it matter?"

"Hell, no," he said, and resumed kissing her with a passion that left no doubt as to his desire for her—or hers for him.

"ARE YOU SURE Tweety Bird will be okay?"

"He'll be fine, honey."

Early Saturday morning, and Sam was taking the goshawk into the mountains to release him. Lyndsey and Gus were along for the ride. They sat in the rear seat. Annie rode up front with him, brightening his mood.

Tweety Bird was in the truck bed, closed inside a spare dog crate Annie had procured. He wasn't in a good mood. But he would be soon.

"What if he gets hurt again?" Lyndsey asked.

"He won't."

"You can't promise that."

Annie shot him a you-should-know-better look.

"You're right," he admitted. "I can't."

Lyndsey had been pestering Sam nonstop since Dr. Murry pronounced Tweety Bird healed and ready for reintroduction into the wild. She was convinced the hawk would meet with misfortune again.

"Tweety Bird is used to living in the mountains," Annie told her. "He's not happy in a chicken coop."

"But we take care of him. We give him raw hamburger."

"He misses flying. He misses hunting for his food. He misses other goshawks. He misses his home." Her demeanor gentled. "Sometimes, wild animals are so miserable in captivity that they let themselves waste away and die. You wouldn't want that."

Sam glimpsed his daughter in the rearview mirror. Her small chin trembled.

Dammit. Maybe he should stop the truck and give her the reassurance she longed for. His poor daughter dreaded loss of any kind, the reminder of her mother's passing too terrible to bear.

He had just started tapping the brake when Gus reached over and gripped Lyndsey's shoulder. "You can't keep Tweety Bird forever. You gotta be tougher."

"Okay." She sniffed, and then nodded. The next instant, the two of them were sharing the pair of earbuds and listening to Lyndsey's MP3 player.

Sam quietly fumed. That was it? One micro pep talk from Gus and Lyndsey was fine. He glanced at Annie. The corners of her mouth quirked with suppressed amusement.

He cut his eyes to the rear seat and muttered in a low voice, "Should I be jealous?"

She laughed then, warm and rich enough to cause a familiar stirring inside him. "You're her dad. No one will ever replace you."

"Right." He wasn't reassured. Gus had wormed his way into a place in Lyndsey's heart Sam thought belonged exclusively to him.

"You can't keep Lyndsey forever," she said, echoing Gus. "You gotta be tougher."

"But she's only eight. Surely I have a few more years."

"They'll go quickly."

"That's what I'm afraid of."

"Me, too."

They shared a look, a slight brushing of their fingers across the seat. It wasn't their first that day. Or even their first that week. Something had changed recently. Sam recalled the exact moment. It was when Annie had kissed him in the kitchen after her meeting with the contractor. She'd finally let down her defenses.

Thank God.

"I swear I won't let Lyndsey lead Nessa astray." He squeezed Annie's fingers again just to reassure himself they were wrapped in his.

"Nessa's a spitfire. I'm more afraid of her leading Lyndsey astray."

The road gently curved as they climbed the mountain to Grey Rock Point, the place Sam had chosen to release Tweety Bird. The peaks, lush and green, rose up from the ground as if only recently born of the earth, their vibrant color brilliant against a clear blue sky.

If Sam stared at the pristine peaks long enough, he could almost imagine that the fire never happened. With a turn of his head, the illusion was lost. The valley lay below, a scarred wasteland.

Guilt widened the hole in his gut. Would he ever get over it?

A short time later they reached Grey Rock Point and began searching for a place to pull safely off the road and park. When he lowered the tailgate, Tweety Bird greeted him by beating his newly healed wings against the inside of the dog crate.

Sam pulled the crate forward, then donned the thick leather gloves Dr. Murry had recommended he wear for protection against the hawk's sharp talons. "He must know what's about to happen."

Lyndsey tried to peer inside the crate. "I wanna help."

"Careful, honey." Sam eased her back. "We don't know how's he's going to act. He might try to bite you."

Dr. Murry had recommended placing a hood on Tweety Bird. Sam tried his best to find one, but there were no bird hoods in Sweetheart. Annie helped with the release by cracking open the crate door while Sam reached in and grabbed Tweety Bird the way the vet had shown him, taking care not to reinjure him.

The hawk squawked and pecked at Sam's hands—and might have done serious damage if not for the gloves.

Sweat formed on Sam's brow. Getting the hawk out of the crate was definitely harder than getting him in. The instant Tweety Bird sensed the outdoors, he started struggling. Sam barely held on. Then, he couldn't anymore.

The release was far less spectacular than those he'd seen on nature documentaries. He nearly dropped Tweety Bird and was swatted in the face several times with a flapping wing before the hawk managed a clumsy liftoff.

Tweety Bird hung suspended in front of them for several endless moments, gathering the wind beneath his wings. Inch by inch, he rose straight up until he hovered ten feet above their heads.

"Awesome," Gus said.

Well stated, thought Sam, shielding his eyes from the glare of the sun.

All at once, Tweety Bird caught an air stream and rode it higher. Before flying away toward the peaks, he executed two perfect circles.

"Look! He's saying goodbye," Sam said, waving his arm.

"He's saying thank-you." Lyndsey's voice wobbled. "He did want to be free."

Sam knelt and wrapped his daughter in his arms. She returned his hug with all the strength in her small body.

"I love you, Daddy," she whispered.

"Love you, too."

Sam felt a sudden bump.

Gus had wrapped an arm around him and Lyndsey both. "Group hug." Did the kid have to insinuate himself everywhere?

Gus motioned to Annie. "What are you waiting for?"

She bent down and joined them, her arm sliding over Sam's shoulders. All right. He supposed the kid did have his uses.

The mood was considerably more jovial on the drive home.

"Daddy," Lyndsey asked, "when can we visit the wildlife refuge?"

His daughter was ready to give up the kits, too? This was real progress.

"Whenever Annie can take us." He cast her a glance.

"Maybe next weekend. Nessa would probably like to see it, too."

Lyndsey and Gus promptly began making plans.

"You miss Nessa?"

At Sam's question, Annie became quiet. "It's not so hard during the week when Gary has her. I have work to keep me busy. The weekends are tougher."

"Is he still bringing up the custody agreement?"

"Not lately. If the rental house doesn't come through, however, that could change."

"Call me if you get stuck."

"I can fight my own battles, Sam."

"I know you can. But you don't have to."

Her reply was a noncommittal sound. But then, a minute later, she reached across the seat for his hand.

Sam hoped Gus wasn't getting any ideas from watching them and checked the rearview mirror. The boy was wisely keeping his mitts to himself.

When they stopped to drop off Gus at his family's mobile home, Irma made an unexpected offer.

"The day's young. Why don't I watch Lyndsey and you two go for lunch or something?"

Or something?

Sam turned to Annie. "I'm game if you are. Unless you have other plans."

"I don't," Annie answered.

His pulse quickened. "Hungry?"

"Not yet. I was thinking…"

Sam was thinking, too. Probably not the same thing as Annie. "What's that?"

"I haven't been horseback riding in ages."

Riding. Okay. That was doable. "Are you sure?" he asked Irma. "Lyndsey can be a handful."

"What's one more?" Irma shooed them away. "Have fun."

After wrangling a hug and kiss from Lyndsey, Sam left with Annie for the ranch. When he aimed the truck in the direction of the barn, Annie stopped him.

"Actually, if it's all right with you, instead of riding I'd like a tour of the house."

"You've already seen it."

"Not the upstairs. Not the new furniture." She paused. "Not your bedroom."

Sam hit the brakes, harder than he intended. Gravel shot out from beneath the tires.

"Whoa, cowboy," she joked.

He turned toward her, resting his arm on the steering wheel. "Sorry. When you said you wanted to see the upstairs, I immediately…" He faced forward. "Never mind."

"Tell me."

"I'm a guy. You mention anything to do with upstairs and bedrooms, and I get ideas."

"What kind of ideas?"

"Ones that involve you and me and the shades drawn."

"Mmm." She nodded as if deliberating a weighty matter. "Well, can I still see the upstairs?"

"Sure." He turned off the engine and hopped out, capping his overactive imagination.

Annie went ahead of him up the walkway to the porch, where he unlocked the front door. He had only just closed the door behind them when Annie spoke from the bottom of the stairs, her voice low and seductive enough to turn a man's blood to fire.

"Just so you know, when I mentioned seeing the bedroom, I was having ideas, too. About you and me and the shades drawn."

Sam gulped. Then he crossed the room to her and didn't stop until they were toe-to-toe, eyes locked.

Extending her arm, she opened her hand and let her purse drop to the hardwood floor. The thud went straight to his pounding heart.

"Annie." He had to be sure. "This isn't a game for me."

"Me, either." Her chest rose and fell sharply, drawing his attention to the V opening of her shirt and the necklace he'd given her. It rested above a hint of cleavage that had enticed him all morning.

"I want you, make no mistake." He was desperate to touch her. Dying to touch her. Yet, he waited. "I have from my first day here when I saw you standing in this very spot."

"What's stopping you?" She lifted her mouth, everything about her going soft in an unspoken invitation.

His body responded with a will of its own, awakening after a long and dreary dormancy.

"I need to know. Why now? What's changed? I've chased you from day one, and you've resisted me at every step."

She averted her gaze, her expression endearingly shy.

He did touch her then. One finger. Under her chin. And tilted her face toward him. "Tell me."

"Tweety Bird."

"The hawk?"

"When you released him, it was as if something inside me was released, too. I realized I can't let the past rule me anymore."

Sam kissed her then, pulling her into his arms and aligning the entire length of her body with his. She responded with a needy moan that turned him instantly hard.

Upstairs. To his bedroom.

He was distracted the next second when his hands found the hem of her shirt and slipped beneath it. Her skin was warm. No, hot. He fitted his palms to her ribs, and then covered her breasts. She rewarded him with a languid sigh of contentment, her nails digging into the flesh of his shoulders.

She inhaled sharply when he abandoned her mouth to taste her neck. "Show me the new bedroom furniture."

Another minute, and he'd have made love to her on the stairs. "My pleasure."

Hand in hand, they climbed upstairs. At the top, he lifted her into his arms, only to set her down at the doorway to his room. She would have to take the last steps on her own.

"Nice." She smiled approvingly. "How's the mattress?"

"Better than the sagging, creaking sack of rags that used to be in here."

"Good." The look she sent him was utterly devilish. "Show me what I've been missing the last nine years." Yanking her shirt over her head, she entered the room and crossed to the bed. There, she unsnapped her jeans and shimmied out of them. "Care to join me?"

Sam didn't need to be asked twice. He was not only going to show her what she'd been missing the past nine years, he intended to give her a preview of what lay in store for them the rest of their lives.

Chapter Fourteen

Annie had let Sam make love to her.

No, not let him. She'd *initiated* it. In broad daylight. At the Gold Nugget. What had she been thinking?

Only that it was *so* worth it.

She stretched luxuriously across the mussed bedsheets, her limbs still humming from the delicious sensations he'd evoked in her. She and Sam may be guilty of a ton of mistakes, but this wasn't one of them.

"Hey."

At the sound of his voice, she rolled slowly over and greeted him with a lazy smile. "Hey to you, too."

He walked across the room and set two glasses of ice water on the nightstand. "Miss me?"

Oh, yes.

"Wait." She stopped him before he slid into bed with her. "I want to look at you."

Sam had spent several long minutes taking in her naked form earlier. Annie wanted her turn.

He was gorgeous. Broader and more muscled than he'd been as a young man. The dark patch of chest hair was thicker. She'd tested its density by sifting her fingers through the springy curls. His hands, though calloused, were gentle when they'd explored her intimate places and capable of bringing her intense pleasure.

He was also a more patient lover, savoring the journey rather than rushing to its conclusion. She appreciated that last change the most.

He studied her as she gazed her fill, and his body hardened in response, letting her know they weren't done. Annie was all ready for round two. Just not yet.

"Come here." She opened her arms.

Sam must have sensed her desire for closeness and not sex. He lay beside her and wrapped her in his embrace.

"When are you going back to California?" she murmured into his neck.

"What? How did you—"

"Lyndsey told me. She's excited."

"You're not mad?" He brushed her hair with his lips.

"It's a visit. And you have to go, your father-in-law needs you." Unlike the last time, Annie wasn't worried. He was coming back. She knew it and didn't stop to question him.

"Come with me."

"I…" She shut her mouth, considering her options before answering.

Was there any reason she couldn't go? Her refusal the last time had been their undoing.

"For a long weekend, maybe. If I can get the day off work."

"Bring Nessa."

"She'd probably love to see a real live cattle ranch."

Annie sighed and wriggled closer to him. Like that, simple as pie. If they had made these kinds of compromises nine years ago, they might never have broken up.

No purpose in playing the what-if game. They were here now, together. *Very* together.

Soon, construction would begin on the inn. Annie would move her family to more spacious living accommodations. One that allowed pets. And there was Sam.

The pinpoints of light at the end of the tunnel had grown into spotlights.

"You hungry?" Sam asked. "I could make lunch. Throw some sandwiches together."

"Mmm. Tempting." She reached between them and took hold of his erection, which instantly swelled. "More tempting."

He groaned. "You're distracting me."

"That's my plan."

"It's working." He pressed her into the mattress, covering her entire length with his body.

His mouth came down on hers, and she lifted her hips to meet him. Like that, they were lost in each other, unaware of the world around them.

So much for lunch.

Afterward, Annie drifted off, the most content she'd been since before the fire. Sam must have fallen asleep, too, for at the sound of a loud banging on the front door, he suddenly jerked and then sprang out of bed.

"It's Mayor Dempsey's car," he said from the window, and quickly snatched his clothes off the floor.

"You could ignore her." Annie pushed up onto one elbow.

"When has the mayor ever given up easily? She'll drive over to the construction site and find Chas. He knows we're in here."

The knock came again. Louder this time.

"You're probably right."

"Wait here." Fully—and hastily—dressed, Sam gave Annie a quick kiss and hurried downstairs.

She abandoned trying to nap after five minutes. Dressing and freshening up in the bathroom, she debated what to do next. It wasn't as if she and Sam had anything to hide. No reason for her to remain secluded upstairs.

Even so, she took the stairs slowly and quietly, wincing each time a step creaked. At the bottom, she noticed Sam had picked up her purse from the floor and hung it on the banister. Voices, Sam's and the mayor's, drifted through the house from the kitchen. They were discussing reservations—Sam had received several more apparently. He hadn't mentioned that to Annie. The mayor was obviously excited and telling him about her ideas for the grand reopening celebration.

"I was thinking, the couple who wins the contest would be guests of the entire town. They'd stay here, get married in the Yeungs' wedding chapel, and we'd host a reception at the Paydirt. All free of charge."

"It sounds great."

"If all goes well, the couple would bring along their family and friends. And the publicity will generate more tourists. I have connections all over the state. TV stations, newspapers, professional organizations. I'll get them to spread the word."

"Count me in."

"I knew you'd say that," the mayor gushed. "Sam, you're the best thing to happen to this town in years. Decades."

"I wouldn't go that far." There was an odd quality to Sam's voice.

Annie wondered if he was thinking of the fire and the orders he didn't disobey. She continued toward the kitchen, only to halt at the mayor's next words.

"I'd go that far and more. The Gold Nugget is the new heart of Sweetheart."

What was Mayor Dempsey saying? Annie's family's inn had always held that honor. And would again.

Pain, razor-sharp, sliced through her.

"Mayor, it isn't," Sam insisted.

"Don't be so modest."

Spinning on her heels, Annie raced back upstairs to the bedroom.

Sam found her perched on the end of the mattress ten minutes later, staring into space. The distant sound of a car engine let her know the mayor was leaving.

"I didn't think she'd ever stop talking." He sat beside Annie. "Though some of her ideas are actually good."

"I heard." She lacked the courage to look him in the face.

"You did?"

"I came downstairs and overheard part of your conversation. I wasn't eavedropping."

"Why didn't you join us?"

Finally, she met his gaze. "She called the ranch the new heart of Sweetheart."

Sam let out a long breath. "She did do that."

"Apparently she's unaware construction on the inn is starting soon."

"You know how the mayor is." He took her hand in his and rested both on her knee. "She was in politician mode. Rallying the troops. She wasn't thinking about what she was saying."

"Or, it's what she believes."

"Annie girl. Please. Don't let her upset you. It's not worth it. You'll rebuild the inn, and it'll be full of guests. Six months at the most. Not everyone who comes to Sweetheart will want to stay at a working cattle ranch."

He was right. But the mayor's slight still stung like a betrayal. Another deserter on a growing list of deserters.

"Instead of letting her get to you—" Sam released her hand to cup her cheek "—prove her wrong. When construction's done, she'll be coming to you, begging you to include the inn in her latest promotion scheme."

She would, too. The design was wonderful.

"I'm being childish," Annie confessed.

"No, you're not." He kissed her, a light brush of his lips across hers. "And, truthfully, I should have defended you more. I got derailed by her excitement. She has that effect on people."

"The contest is a good idea. For you, for the town, for everyone."

He kissed her again. By the third one, Annie was mostly over her hurt. She had only herself and her family to worry about. Mayor Dempsey had the entire population of Sweetheart, and she would do what was best for them.

Besides, Sam had a point. The Hennessys' turn to reign over Sweetheart would come again. Annie would count the days.

"How 'bout I buy you that lunch before I take you home?" he asked.

"Anyplace but the Paydirt. Yes, I'm being petty."

"Who cares if you are?"

She laughed then, her mood mostly restored.

Rather than dine out, they decided on making sandwiches. Annie fixed a quick salad to round out the meal. Chopping lettuce and tomatoes and setting the table went slow with Sam constantly interrupting her for a kiss or a squeeze from behind.

They were chatting over the last bites when her cell phone rang, the chime carrying from the parlor.

"Do you mind?" She was already rising from the table. "It could be Gary. Nessa was fighting the sniffles when he picked her up yesterday."

"Don't worry about it."

The call had gone to voice mail by the time she fished her phone from her purse. She read the number as she returned to the kitchen, her brow knit in confusion.

"Everything okay?" Sam asked. He was carting the empty dishes and plates to the sink.

"It's the architect. Why would he be calling me on a Saturday?"

"He's in town today. At least, he was earlier. Consulting with a new client."

Annie listened to his message. "He says to give him a call when I have a minute."

"Go ahead. I'll finish the dishes."

Annie hit Redial, an unexplained anxiety squeezing her middle. She had no reason to assume the worst, yet she did.

The architect picked up almost immediately. "Hi, Annie. Hope I didn't interrupt your day off."

"Not at all." She pulled out a chair and slid into it. "What's up?"

"I have the soil test results. The firm emailed me a copy late yesterday. I apologize, I've been so busy I didn't check my account until now."

"How do they look?"

"Is there a chance we can get together today?"

His tone put her even more on edge. "What's wrong?"

"It might be better if we discussed this in person."

"Please." Her fingers tightened on the phone. She was aware Sam had come over to stand by her. "I have to know."

"The results aren't good. There are high levels of contamination. The soil can be treated, but it'll be expensive and time-consuming."

"How much?"

"Hard to say for certain without getting a quote from the engineer."

"Give me a rough estimate."

The amount he stated was more than a third of the entire insurance settlement.

"I can deliver a hard copy of the report when we meet."

She barely heard the rest of what he said. It was lost in the thick fog that had come from nowhere to swallow her.

"THERE ARE GOVERNMENT grants you can apply for," Sam said.

"We've already looked into those. It's a paperwork nightmare and takes forever. Plus, there's no guarantee."

"Might be worth it." He glanced over at Annie.

She stared listlessly out the passenger side window of his truck, avoiding him. She'd avoided him since the architect delivered the devastating news about the soil test results.

Déjà vu.

She'd been like this before, withdrawing into herself. The

first had been the night he told her he was taking a job in California. The second, when they broke up for good a year later. He wasn't sure he could handle a third time.

At some point, Annie had to trust him completely. Trust them. If she didn't, their chances of making it were slim.

"Let me pay for the soil treatment."

Indignation flashed in her eyes. "I won't take your money."

His *late wife's* money, as she'd pointed out. "I wouldn't expect you to. Consider it a loan."

"No."

"You can pay me interest."

"I'll figure this out on my own."

"That's just it. You don't have to. We can be in this together if you let me."

"It's not together if you're pulling all the weight."

He turned onto her street and parked in front of her apartment. Annie bailed out of his truck. So did Sam. He followed her inside even though no invitation was issued.

"I didn't mean to insult you," he said.

"You didn't."

She threw her things down on the coffee table and gave a huge sigh of exasperation. Or, was it despair?

The apartment was empty, and Sam was glad for small favors. Annie would talk more openly if they were alone.

He took out his cell phone and called Irma, asking if Lyndsey could stay a little longer. Annie watched him during the entire conversation, not hiding her misery.

"I know the results weren't what you expected," he said, disconnecting from Irma.

"You think?" She folded her arms protectively across her middle.

She might have turned her back to him but he went over and placed a hand on her shoulder.

"We can figure this out. It's going to take a little longer, sure, and a little more money. But, it's not impossible."

"Why does everything come down to money?" She pulled away from him and flung herself onto the sofa, covering her face with her hands. "I hate wallowing in self-pity."

"You have a right to wallow." He sat down beside her. "Let me help."

"Stop saying that," she snapped. "You can't fix everything by whipping out your checkbook."

Silence hung between them. Lingered.

"Not everything." Reining in his impatience, Sam broke the lull. "But I can make this right. What's the difference between borrowing money from me and from a bank?"

"I don't sleep with the bank."

"Wow." Stunned by her insensitivity, he sat back, telling himself her remark was a product of her frustration and disappointment and not a stab at him. "I didn't make the offer because we're lovers. I made it because we're friends. Because I care."

She scrubbed her cheeks. "I do appreciate it even if I sound ungrateful."

"Then take it."

"I can't."

"The money's not Trisha's. It's mine."

"Try and understand." She shook her head. "I've lost so much these last few months. I'm hanging on by a thread, and that thread is mighty fragile some days. You, on the other hand, have it all. As if you're scooping up everything I've lost. My dream of owning the Gold Nugget. My mother. Our former employees." Her posture sagged. "The Hennessys' place in the community. Imagine how that makes me feel."

"Imagine how I feel. All I've done is try to help you, and your response every single time is to throw it back at me. As if my offer's worthless. I don't deserve that."

"You don't." She grimaced and pressed her palm to her chest. "I'm hurting, Sam, and I'm afraid I won't ever stop."

"Mayor Dempsey shouldn't have said that about the ranch."

"But she did, and it's true. You're practically single-handedly bringing this town back from the brink of extinction." She straightened, though it wasn't with determination. "Sometimes I think the universe is trying to send me a message. I shouldn't rebuild the inn."

"If you won't borrow the money from me, then let me co-sign a bank loan with you."

"Why do you want to help me so badly?"

"I told you. To put the settlement money to good use."

"You can't buy off guilt, Sam."

Another stab, this one a direct hit in the heart. "Is that what you think I'm doing?"

"Kind of, yeah."

He tensed. "I didn't cause the fire. And even if I'd disobeyed orders, I couldn't have prevented it from ravaging Sweetheart. Not alone or even with my crew. You helped me realize that."

"I wasn't talking about the fire."

"Leaving you when I did, then. Okay, I could have done a better job delivering the news about taking the job in California. Called more frequently. Returned for visits."

"That, too." Her look implied he'd yet to hit the nail on the head.

"Trisha."

"Let's face it. You and I, we weren't the best of spouses. We married for reasons other than a deep and abiding love, which should be the only one. You feel responsible for Trisha's death. It's obvious when you talk about her. Her death and Lyndsey losing her mother. And I feel responsible for my failed marriage."

"I have guilt. Who wouldn't? Had I been a better husband, a more devoted husband, a more attentive husband, she wouldn't have strayed. Not been in that car when the drunk driver plowed into her at thirty miles over the speed limit."

Sam hadn't realized how loud his voice had risen until it echoed back at him from the walls.

"It's noble of you to spend the settlement money on others," she said. "And generous."

"But not noble if I spend it on you. Then it's…something else. A payoff for services rendered."

"I'm probably too independent for my own good."

Sam's temper snapped. "I'm so tired of hearing you say that. You, your mother and your grandmother wave your independence like some banner of glory when what you really do is use it as an excuse not to get close to the men who love you."

"That isn't true."

"No? Look at all three of you. Love has to be on your terms or not at all."

She shot to her feet. "If you're trying to convince me to take the loan, you're doing a terrible job."

"I've done everything, bent over backward for you. Hell, put you before my own daughter and father-in-law, the best friend I have. It's still not enough. For God's sake, Annie, what more do I have to do to prove myself? Until you stop punishing me for leaving you?"

Shock widened her eyes. "I'm not punishing you."

"Sure seems like it."

She hugged herself, and in that instant, she looked as young as her own daughter. "I'm scared, Sam. How do I know you won't leave again?"

"Lyndsey loves it here. I'm not taking her away."

"And you?"

"I love it here, too, Annie."

If she read between the lines, she gave no indication. "You're returning to California."

"For a month at the most."

"You could change your mind. You've done it before."

Anger surged inside him. He removed his hat and threw it on the coffee table next to Annie's things. "I'm at my wit's end. I don't know what to do. I admit it, I screwed up when we were younger. But you have to quit holding it against me."

"And you have to quit holding my one mistake against me. I lost faith in you, and I did start seeing Gary while we were technically together."

He shoved his fingers through his hair, taking a moment to compose himself. "I understand you're going through a rough patch. Been there, done that."

"Losing everything is a lot more than a rough patch."

"Which is why I've tried to help."

"Sometimes it feels like your offers are just your way of placating me."

"What?" That was the furthest thing from his mind.

"You don't think I should rebuild the inn. I can tell."

"I think you should reconsider, yes. Especially in light of the soil contamination. Especially when you don't have to rebuild."

"I do have to rebuild. For my family. You know that. They're *all* I think about. I've made every sacrifice for them."

Sam couldn't believe they'd gone from making incredible love just two hours ago to an all-out blowup. Yet, they had.

"At least you still have your family," he said. "Given the choice, I'd have sacrificed my home and job for Trisha any day. For Lyndsey's sake."

"This isn't a game of comparing who's lost the most or who's the most miserable."

"You're right. That was low of me."

"We need to stop squabbling and act like adults." She rubbed her cheeks and sighed heavily. "What if we've rushed into this…you and me…too quickly?"

"Are you saying you want to take a step back?"

"I'm saying, instead of Nessa and I flying out to California, maybe we should use the time you're away to reevaluate. You might decide to stay there after all and be a long-distance owner of the Gold Nugget."

"What do you want?"

She didn't answer right away. When she did, she was probably the most honest she'd been since they started arguing.

"What if I never get my old life back? What then?"

"The new one might be better."

"I have so little left. I can't take that chance right now."

Was *he* so little?

"You're pushing me away again, and I'm tired of it, Annie."

"I might be doing that. And not to play the comparing game again, but your loss is older than mine and your recovery time longer. I'm still grieving and I'm not ready for you to come in here and rescue me like some knight in shining armor. I've got to heal on my own."

Annie didn't want him. Not in her corner. Not in her life.

"Guess I'm wasting my time here." He rose and grabbed his hat. Yes, he was acting surly by walking out. Still, he couldn't stop himself. "I have to pick up Lyndsey. I'll see you later. Let me know if you need anything either before I leave or while I'm gone. But we both know you won't ask."

"Sam." She reached for him. "Earlier today, it was the most incredible day I've had in…years, I guess."

She waited till now to tell him?

"Goodbye." He didn't look back as he left the apartment. If he had, she'd see how completely her rejection devastated him.

Annie wasn't the only one who'd had the most incredible day in years.

For Sam, it was also one of the worst.

Chapter Fifteen

Annie dropped to the ground amid the rubble that had once been her home, her life, her security.

Her first love.

Sobs racked her entire body. At last. She'd staved them off for months, refusing to yield even when the fire officials delivered the news that the inn was gone. Especially then. Hard as it was, she'd maintained control. For her family, for her friends in town and for herself.

Now, tears fell freely into the hands that covered her face. An outpouring of pain, for which there seemed no end.

Was she being *too* independent, as Sam had accused during their fight? So much so that she pushed people away? Sabotaged any chance she and Sam—she and anyone—had for a relationship?

Oh, God. She was.

With her grandmother's bouts of confusion, her mother's depression and her daughter being completely dependent, Annie had seen no other alternative than to bear the entire weight of their misfortune alone.

And she hadn't forsaken that burden for anything. Including a future with Sam.

One week. A decade-long week. Without even a single glimpse of him. What if she'd accepted his offer to loan her the money for the soil treatment instead of refusing?

She'd be here now, rejoicing. Preparing to move into a new place. Not falling apart.

Annie didn't lose everything in the fire. But she had now. Not lost. Thrown away.

According to her mother, Sam and Lyndsey were departing for California in a matter of days. He'd return but Fiona said it would be without Lyndsey. Sam was making his home base in California instead of Sweetheart.

History was repeating itself, all right. Annie had pretty much guaranteed that. Fresh tears fell.

She didn't try to stop them. This crying jag was long overdue. Eventually, however, it subsided. Only because she ran out of energy. Wiping her eyes, she realized she was kneeling in one of the few bare patches the engineering company had left behind after the soil tests.

Contamination. Due to toxins. The hardwood floors her grandmother had commissioned to be built and the chemicals used to treat them would be responsible. Plus asbestos in the basement and attic. With a building as old as the inn, there could be countless other culprits, like lead paint and fertilizer in the storage shed.

She covered her face with her hands. What now? She had no choice but to hire Chas's construction company to clear the land. The debris couldn't be left to rot indefinitely. It was a health hazard as well as unsightly. And guests staying at the Gold Nugget...

The reminder of Sam's success launched a fresh wave of misery. She was happy for him. Happy for the town. Happy for the people he'd employed, including her mother.

Annie had kept her family fed, clothed and sheltered. But it was her mother who'd enabled them to improve their standard of living. Thanks entirely to Sam.

Really, Annie was happy. Even though anyone stumbling across her at this moment would think differently.

"Hello! Annie?"

"Over here." She quickly used the hem of her uniform shirt to blot her cheeks, then finger combed her hair.

"There you are." Granny Orla poked her head through the opening that had once been the inn's front door. "Are you all right? You look awful."

"I'm fine."

"Have another run-in with Gary?"

"Not at all."

"Must be Sam then."

"Why do you automatically assume it's Sam?" She hadn't mentioned anything to her family, preferring to avoid their questions.

"I've seen that look on your face before."

"What are you doing here?" Annie removed her sunglasses from her shirt pocket and donned them. "And who brought you, by the way?"

Her first visit to the inn in two weeks, and she'd been interrupted by her grandmother. What were the odds?

A hundred percent, apparently.

"I came to look for my book."

Oh, that again. Granny's fixation with her phantom book was growing old. Annie wasn't in the mood today. "Where's Mom?"

"At home with Nessa."

"She didn't bring you?"

"Heavens, no. She's fixing dinner. A real dinner. Pot roast. Been nice having her take an interest in cooking again. Fiona's a culinary genius. Don't know where she got it. Certainly not from me. Maybe her father. Though that man never fried an egg or toasted a piece of bread that I ever saw. But, Lord, he was a handsome devil."

Her grandmother was rambling again.

"Granny, don't tell me you walked here."

"Certainly not. Irma's daughter gave me a lift."

"Carrie only has her learner's permit. Was Irma in the car, too?"

"Irma's at the chapel. Helping Wanda with sorting through all the things they've collected. Have you been there lately? The basement is crammed to the ceiling in some places."

Annie refused to be sidetracked. "Granny, Irma's daughter can't drive without a licensed adult in the car with her."

"I'm a licensed adult."

"You haven't driven for five years."

"I don't think that matters."

There was no reasoning with her. "Come on, let's go."

"Not till I find my book." She started across what had been the lobby, picking her way carefully and with surprising agility for a woman her age.

"Fine. I'll help." With no other option, Annie accompanied her grandmother. "Where's the last place you remember seeing it?"

That ought to be a trick question.

Only her grandmother didn't hesitate. "On a shelf in the sitting room."

Their private rooms had been on the first floor. Fiona's was off the kitchen. Granny Orla had used a small room near the downstairs bathroom. The sitting room was adjacent to that. Annie started out, the mountains of debris not hindering her in the least. She instinctively knew the layout of the inn.

"This is where the sitting room was."

Nothing recognizable of it remained. Any furnishing or contents were buried beneath tons of wreckage from the second story and the roof.

"Oh, dear."

Annie spun at the sounds of distress coming from her grandmother. The older woman was trembling. Her hands covered her mouth, and her eyes were red and moist.

She went to her grandmother, who looked to have shrunk in the past few minutes, and rubbed her back, praying she wouldn't drift off into confusion. If she wasn't already half-way there.

"Don't worry yourself," she assured Annie. "I'm fine."

"If your book's here, there's no way we can find it."

"We certainly can't find it if we don't look."

Annie resigned herself to digging through the muck and mess. For a little while.

"Let me get my gloves and a shovel from the SUV. I don't want you touching anything while I'm gone. You hear me, Granny?"

"I'm not deaf."

Granny, of course, went right ahead with her search, touching everything. When Annie returned, she found her grandmother bent over, attempting to lift a heavy plank and, Annie was convinced, give herself a heart attack.

"Wait. Let me do that."

Granny ignored Annie, demonstrating that the Hennessy stubborn gene had originated with her.

Annie forcibly removed the plank from Granny's hands, lifted it and shoved it aside. The plank fell with a mighty thud, shooting clouds of black ash into the air.

Granny gasped, and then coughed. Annie covered her nose with her arm. If only she'd brought face masks. They worked for twenty minutes, discovering an old watch, completely useless, various TV components and an antique oil-lamp base that was in reasonably decent condition.

"I'm tired, Granny, and it's getting late." Annie leaned on the shovel for support. Every bare inch of her skin was coated in grim. "Let's call it a day."

"What's this?" Granny Orla knelt, lifted the end of what looked like part of a metal shelving unit and reached underneath.

"Granny, stop. You'll hurt yourself."

"I think I found it!"

Impossible. "Trust me, nothing made of paper and cardboard could survive this." She gestured with her hand.

"Help me," Granny implored.

Annie seized the shelving unit. After this, they were out of here. Even if she had to drag her grandmother kicking and screaming. She was too physically and emotionally exhausted to continue.

If only Nessa wasn't with her father this weekend. Annie craved the special comfort her daughter provided.

"Lord Almighty," Granny exclaimed, tugging on a bulky object. "It's my book."

She couldn't have found it. Annie heaved the shelving unit aside, which made a terrible clatter when it fell. Then she went over to her grandmother—who did indeed hold a large square object.

Annie removed her sunglasses and stared, unblinking. Granny let out a wistful sigh and cradled the book to her bosom.

No, not a book. A photo album. And it appeared intact! How could that be?

Slowly, Annie lowered herself onto the ground beside her grandmother, a strange sensation coursing through her.

"What's in it?"

"Our history."

Granny cracked open the cover on the photo album. Charred flakes fell like snow. Though the outside was badly burned, by some miracle, the inside had sustained little damage.

Memories returned. Annie vaguely recalled seeing this album when she was a child but not since. She'd all but forgotten its existence.

Not her grandmother.

Granny Orla turned page after page. A few of the photographs were scorched. Others merely discolored and their corners curled. Some were almost like new. Could the metal shelving unit have protected the album from the flames? It didn't seem possible.

Yet, here was the proof.

The pictures told the story of the inn, and with it, the Hennessy women. The first ones, over fifty years old and in black and white, were of the wooded lot before construction started. Someone, Annie assumed her grandmother, had taken photos of the inn during each stage. It grew from a plain cement foundation to the building she'd lived in most of her life.

There were pictures of Annie's mother as a child with Granny Orla. Pictures of Annie as a child with her mother. Men Annie didn't recognize.

"Who's that?" she asked, her throat scratchy.

"Your grandfather." Granny Orla gazed at the brown-edged photograph with tenderness. "I told you he was a handsome devil."

Had she loved him? Annie always assumed her grandmother's affections belonged to the star of *The Forty-Niners*.

"Why did he leave?"

"Why do they all leave? We drive them away."

"Mom told me my dad didn't want to settle down. That, according to him, he had to be free."

"He was a wanderer. Like your grandfather."

"Like Sam, too." Annie hadn't noticed the similarities before.

"Sam isn't anything like them. I've yet to meet a more devoted family man."

"Now maybe."

"Always. You were just three steps ahead of him and unwilling to wait."

Granny Orla's words hit home. "I'm not sure I've changed."

"We all change, sweetie. And we have to move on. Can't stay in one place forever."

She handed over the photo album. As Annie's fingers made

contact with the cover, a chill ran up her spine, and she was once again overcome with amazement.

"I'll carry it to the SUV for you."

"No." Granny covered Annie's hands with hers. "I want you to keep it."

"Granny!"

"I know you'll take good care of it."

"But it's yours."

Granny shook her head. "You're trying so hard to rebuild the inn. Sacrificing so much. More than you should. More than you need to. Have you ever asked yourself what's driving you?"

"The inn is our legacy. It's been in our family for fifty years. I want to pass it on to Nessa."

"Annie, this is your legacy." She squeezed the album. "The Hennessy spirit. We are strong women. We are fighters. We make fulfilling and wonderful lives for ourselves despite all odds. Nessa will, too."

"I suppose I could have the photographs restored and framed."

"I hope you will. But isn't there more you can do with them?"

Another chill ran up her spine. She'd been so focused on rebuilding the inn, she'd missed out on what was really important.

"Maybe. Yes, there is more I can do." She stood and reached out a hand to her grandmother. "Let's go."

"Where?"

The universe had been sending Annie a message. She was finally listening.

"To the chapel."

ANNIE'S FIRST INCLINATION was to chew out Irma for letting her daughter drive Granny to the inn. But the moment they entered the chapel basement, her mind emptied…

…and her heart filled.

Besides Irma and her daughter, Mayor Dempsey was there, along with Wanda and the school principal.

"Can you believe this?" The mayor's gaze traveled the room.

"No." Annie walked a narrow makeshift aisle, the photo album resting in the crook of one arm. "Where did it all come from?"

"Most of it was either saved by the owners or pulled from wreckage. They had nowhere else to store it so they brought it here."

There wasn't a single piece of junk in the place. Each item, from the rooster weather vane that had sat atop the Millers' house and the Welcome to Sweetheart, Nevada sign posted at the town limits, stirred a fond memory.

"I have pictures," she stammered. "Of the inn. Some of them are really old."

"How lucky you saved them."

"We didn't." Annie held the album out for the mayor's inspection.

"We found them," Granny Orla supplied. "Just now. In the ruins."

Mayor Dempsey frowned in puzzlement. "How is that possible?"

"I don't know." Annie nudged open the cover. "Look for yourself."

The mayor wasn't the only one impressed. Everyone crowded close.

"Amazing!"

"Incredible."

There were more gasps of surprise with each turning of the page.

"A metal shelving unit apparently fell on top of the album. It must have shielded it. Granny…" Annie stopped. "How did you know?"

"I had a hunch." She winked. "I'm not as confused as everyone thinks I am." She certainly wasn't acting disoriented anymore.

"What are you going to do with all this stuff?" Annie left the album with the mayor as she perused the room. She let her fingers graze the front of a circular saw blade the size of a tire, wary of its deadly teeth. The saw blade had hung on the wall in the Lumberjack Diner, a reminder of the days when ponderosa pines were harvested to build homes. The Gold Nugget Ranch. Her family's inn. The diner had contained many artifacts from the town's early days. All gone.

No, not all. In addition to the saw blade, Annie recognized an old anvil and a sledgehammer. Pieces of history, reminders of what the town had been like before it was crippled. They deserved to be preserved.

The chills that had started at the inn grew stronger.

"Problem is, we can't keep everything here," Wanda said, looking to the school principal for confirmation. "The Yeungs need the space, what with the tourists starting to return."

"Is there anywhere else you can use for storage?"

Wanda shook her head sadly. "You know what a premium available space is in Sweetheart. It's a shame, too. For some, these items are all that's left of their home or business."

Like Granny's photo album and the other small treasures Annie had recovered from the inn ruins.

"If there was only some way to preserve everything for posterity," Annie mused. "Where everyone could view them."

"Don't forget the pictures." The mayor closed the album and returned it to Granny. "I have dozens of the town, going back every bit as far as these and further. I even have a tintype of my great-great-great-grandfather. He was one of the original settlers in Sweetheart."

"There's the photographs at Sam's ranch, too," Irma added. "Of *The Forty-Niners* show."

Interesting how the Gold Nugget had become Sam's ranch.

He was now an integral part of the town, and he probably didn't realize it. If he did, would he change his mind and move here permanently?

"We need a place," the mayor reflected. "A central location."

"What if we convert one of the old empty buildings into a museum of sorts." *The Sweetheart Museum,* Annie thought. *The Sweetheart Memorial!*

An homage to the town before the fire. Surely, there were many, many more antiques and artifacts people had saved or salvaged. Things they'd be willing to donate in exchange for safekeeping.

"Why not?" Her question was met with a roomful of blank stares.

"Where would we locate an old building?" the mayor asked.

"Annie." Granny Orla came closer. "What's going through that head of yours?"

She smiled at her grandmother. "The inn."

"Display all this at the new inn?"

"No. Build the memorial on the site of the inn." She quickly calculated the numbers in her head.

After covering the cost of the soil treatment, there would be enough money left over from the insurance company to construct a simple structure. Perhaps reminiscent of the original inn. Glass cases could be designed for the more fragile pieces, like clothing and china. Wooden stands for the hardier ones.

The more her idea took hold, the more her excitement mounted. Words tumbled out in a rush as she tried to explain.

"My God, Annie," Mayor Dempsey said when she was done. "What a marvelous undertaking."

"But would tourists really care about our history and what the town was like before the fire?" the principal asked.

"It wouldn't be for the tourists," Annie insisted. "Not entirely. It would be for us. So our children could learn about their heritage and what their parents went through. Why we fought tooth and nail to save this town."

Granny Orla gripped Annie's hand firmly in hers. "Are you sure? You've had your heart set on rebuilding the inn."

She couldn't explain it. She only knew that constructing a memorial on the former site of the inn was the right course.

"I'm sure, Granny. But it's really up to you. The deed's in your name."

"I can't think of a better or more fitting use for that land."

Granny Orla's eyes weren't the only damp ones in the room. Even Irma's daughter was a little emotional.

The group stayed and brainstormed for another half hour, until well after dark. It was agreed they'd form a committee, headed by the mayor, and individuals were recommended for recruitment. Annie and her family would be in charge of the construction, and the memorial would be dedicated to the Hennessys. Mayor Dempsey wouldn't hear of anything else.

When Annie and Granny Orla left, they took the album with them. They would have the photographs restored as best as possible and framed. In the meantime, Annie wanted to show the album to Nessa.

She was too young to understand its importance. Someday, however, she would. And she'd carry on the Hennessy legacy, like her mother, grandmother and great-grandmother before her.

Chapter Sixteen

Sam was still in Sweetheart. Eight days since he'd last seen Annie. Since their blowup.

Why hadn't he left for California yet? The fall cattle roundup was scheduled to start next week, and he'd promised his father-in-law.

Easy. He didn't want to go without seeing Annie.

Running out of excuses and unable to keep stalling, he'd instructed Irma on what to pack. He and Lyndsey had visited the wildlife refuge the day before and surrendered the raccoon kits. His poor, sweet daughter had cried the entire way there and the entire way back. And he feared the worst was yet to come.

As much as she loved her grandfather, she didn't want to leave Sweetheart. Not forever. The prospect of future visits didn't lessen her misery.

Sam stood on the front porch, watching Gus and his younger siblings play a game of tag. Lyndsey sat off to the side, distancing herself. Par for the course. Between the kits and moving soon, she'd been moping round the clock.

Beyond them, in front of the barn, Will led a group of five guests on the ranch's first official trail ride, the horses walking nose to tail. Their destination: observing the sunset from Potato Hill.

Sam indulged in a moment of self-satisfaction. His goal of

owning a working guest ranch had become a reality. Reservations weren't exactly pouring in, only a handful each week. That would change soon.

The heart of Sweetheart.

He'd never imagined stealing that title from Annie and her family. Never wanted it. When he objected, the mayor persevered. Promotion was well underway for the free wedding and reception and advance interest was exceeding expectations. Annie had to be hurting.

He'd heard from Irma who'd heard from Fiona that Annie was burying herself in her work. Just like when the inn had burned. Her family was worried. Sam, too. He'd talk to her if he thought it might help, but he doubted she'd take his call.

Was that the only reason he hadn't checked on her? Hell, no.

Avoidance was a tactic he'd relied heavily on after Trisha died. A tactic the grief counselor warned him against.

"Hey, kids," Sam called, interrupting their play. "Time for evening chores. Who wants to help?"

"Me, me!" It was Gus, not Lyndsey, who answered.

Sam strolled over to her. "What's wrong, honey?"

"Where's Annie?"

"Probably at work. Why?"

"Why didn't she come with us to the wildlife refuge? She said she would.

"She's busy."

"She hasn't been here for days." Lyndsey's voice was ripe with accusation. "You and she had a fight."

"Who told you?"

Her glance went straight to Gus. Sam glowered at him.

The boy wasn't intimidated. "My mom blabbed. Ms. Hennessy figured it out."

Fiona.

Sam groaned. "Let's talk about this later, okay?"

Lyndsey acted as if she hadn't heard him. "It's not fair.

She was my friend, too. And you messed it up. Now we're leaving, and I won't ever see her again."

Oh, boy. He hadn't seen this coming. "I'm sure Annie will visit if you ask her."

"No, she won't. She's mad at you."

"She's not mad." Not exactly.

Gus shook his head disgustedly.

Sam refused to defend himself to a pair of eight-year-olds.

"How could you?" Lyndsey demanded, her fists clenched at her sides.

What he heard was, *How could you make another mistake? Drive another important person away? Wreck my life?*

"It's complicated, honey. And hard to explain."

"You don't have to explain it to me. You just need to make up with her. Tell her you're sorry. So we don't have to move back to California."

"We're not moving because Annie and I had a fight. Your grandpa needs me for the fall roundup—"

Lyndsey stormed off to the barn, Gus and his siblings hot on her heels.

Sam remained, rooted in place. Could he make up with Annie? Did he want to? He certainly didn't like the way they'd left things.

An empty lumber truck drove past the house and down the drive, having unloaded its shipment. With the cement foundations on the new cabins poured, framing had started. Before long, two months at most, Sam and Lyndsey could reside in their deluxe cabin. For a visit.

Or longer. Lyndsey did love it here. Sam, too.

But Annie might not want him living in Sweetheart full-time. A town this size, bumping into each other was inevitable.

Maybe he should hunt down Chas at the construction site and pump him for information. Soil treatment at the inn had started. Sam noticed the equipment and temporary fencing that morning when he'd driven past en route to the general store. Annie was finally rebuilding the inn. Without his help.

He'd just decided to walk over to the new cabins when Irma opened the front door and beckoned him inside, delight showing on her plain face. A welcome change after Lyndsey's constant sour expression.

"Come see what I found," Irma said before he'd reached the porch.

She scurried ahead of him, across the parlor and up the stairs, taking him to the tiny third bedroom that wasn't being used. A tattered cardboard box lay in the middle of the empty floor.

"I was cleaning in here, haven't given it a thorough top to bottom yet, when I found this on the closet shelf, shoved clear in the back."

"What's in it?" He lifted one of the flaps.

"Film reels. From the show."

Glimpsing the contents, Sam knelt beside the box, his heart beating faster.

Irma bent at the waist and braced her hands on her knees. "I took a quick peek, then came running to fetch you."

He was almost afraid to pick up the fragile, dust-covered film reels for fear they'd break. Curiosity overruled caution, and he removed the top one. It felt sturdier than it looked.

"They must have been in there all along. Forty years or more," Irma continued. "Aren't those pictures underneath?"

There were indeed photographs. Black-and-whites. A hundred at least. Sam dug carefully beneath the reels and extracted two. They featured the show's main cast members, including Granny Orla's lover, wearing street clothes. They were lounging in front of the ranch house, having a laugh, their handsome faces split by generous smiles.

"I wonder what's on the reels?" Irma's hushed voice echoed in the empty room.

"Outtakes, maybe. Unused footage."

"Must be worth a fortune."

"I doubt it. Probably worth no more than sentimental value. If the film is even viewable."

Sam considered the benefits of having it restored. Once they reopened the house for tours, visitors might enjoy watching the old footage on a closed-circuit TV. And the photographs could be added to the ones already hanging on the walls. Unless...

He flipped over one of the pictures. No name, no copyright stamp. Would that be a problem? Could they legally display the photos or show the film without permission?

"I'm going to have our secretary in California do some investigating. Try and locate anyone involved in the production of *The Forty-Niners*." Another task to complete when he returned.

"Isn't that Granny Orla?" Irma exclaimed.

"You're right."

Sam extracted the photo Irma was pointing at. The glowingly happy young woman could be none other than Annie's grandmother. She was wrapped in the arms of the TV star. The grainy quality and weathered finish of the photo didn't diminish the fact they were head over heels in love.

"Whatever happened to him?" Sam mused aloud.

"His wife took ill right after the series wrapped up. Breast cancer, they say. Terminal. He went home to Hollywood to be with her."

"I didn't realize he was married."

"It wasn't a secret. Not really. Supposedly he and his wife had an arrangement. They were both stars and married because it benefitted their careers. After she passed, he came back and begged Granny Orla to marry him. She said no."

"Why? Was she afraid of a scandal?"

"Like that would have bothered Granny." Irma harrumphed. "She didn't want to leave Sweetheart. You know how those Hennessy women are. Married to the inn." She abruptly slapped a hand over her mouth. "Sorry about that, Sam. No offense."

"None taken. From what I've heard, men who love the Hennessy women don't tend to stick around long."

"It's the curse."

"Do you really believe that nonsense?"

"Must be some reason none of them has married their true love."

Break it. Break the curse.

Sam suddenly wanted that more than his next breath. But Annie would have to want to break the curse, too.

"Have you heard about the Sweetheart Memorial?" Irma asked, straightening.

"The what?" Sam rose, balancing the box of film reels in his arms.

"I wondered if Annie mentioned it to you. She's building a memorial to the town. On her family's land."

Sam almost dropped the box. "What about the inn?"

"They decided not to rebuild."

"Not rebuild?" How could that be? The inn meant the world to Annie.

He needed to see her. Right away. Hammer some sense into her. If she'd even agree to see him.

Irma waited for him at the top of the stairs. "They already have a huge collection for the memorial. At the chapel. You should see it. Mayor Dempsey's formed a committee. If you don't want all those pictures and film reels, I'm sure the committee would."

"Is Annie by chance on the committee?"

"Course. She's in charge of construction."

And the committee might want the film reels.

"You know, Irma, that's a really great suggestion." Sam felt better than he had in eight days. "Remind me to give you a raise."

"Won't hear me object." She practically danced down the

stairs ahead of him. "I'll take the box for you. I'm stopping by the chapel on the way home. Me and Carrie are both helping out. Annie will be by later, too."

Irma's suggestion was getting better by the minute.

"Not necessary. I'll do it and meet you there."

In the kitchen, Sam checked the time. Annie would be off work soon.

"If you don't need me anymore," Irma said, "I'll grab my kids and head home."

"They're in the barn. I'll go with you."

Sam stopped first at his truck and loaded the box. In the barn, Irma collected her children, leaving Sam and Lyndsey alone. She was cleaning out the goats' stall. Sylvester the cat observed from atop a grain barrel.

Sam liked having all the animals around. The only one missing was a dog.

There were plenty of dogs at the ranch in California. They could bring one back with them—if they were to settle here for good.

"Hey, there."

Lyndsey continued to ignore him. She might only be a child but she could hold a grudge with the best of them.

"I thought maybe you'd like to take a trip with me."

"Where?" she asked grumpily without looking up.

"To the Sweetheart Memorial. To see Annie." He grabbed the empty kits' cage, which leaned against the wall. "And return this."

That got her attention. And the smile he'd been waiting for. Sam was smiling pretty wide himself.

"SAM! HELLO." PLEASURE resounded in Mayor Dempsey's voice.

Startled, Annie dropped the polishing cloth she'd been using. As of yesterday, she might have resented Sam's unexpected appearance in the chapel basement. Instead, a jolt of anticipation raced through her, reminding her of the day he'd returned to Sweetheart.

Of the first time they'd met.

Finding the photo album and deciding to use the insurance settlement for a memorial had changed her perspective. About a lot of things.

She loved Sam. Had always loved him. Marriage to Gary changed nothing. Neither had losing the inn or Sam buying the Gold Nugget.

Annie was like all the Hennessy women, utterly and completely devoted to one man. For her grandmother, it had been the TV star. For her mother, it was Annie's father.

She rose and set aside the leather horse collar she'd been cleaning. What was Sam doing here anyway? And he'd brought Lyndsey with him.

The girl ran over to Annie, only to stop short a few feet in front of her.

"Are you mad at me, too?" she asked in a small voice.

"Why would you ever think that?" Annie opened her arms.

Lyndsey flew into them. "Can I call you when I'm in California?"

"As often as you want."

"We brought some stuff for the memorial."

"Oh?" Annie hadn't noticed Sam holding a cardboard box. She'd seen only him.

Their gazes connected, and she tried to gauge what lay behind his. He revealed little. Funny, she was usually the guarded one.

"Can I look around?" Lyndsey asked.

"Sure, just be careful and don't touch anything without permission."

"Come along, dear." Granny took charge of Lyndsey.

Which left Annie with no barriers between her and Sam. He continued to stare at her to the point where Annie became self-conscious.

"If I were you," Granny whispered loudly from across two crowded tables, "I wouldn't let that man get away for a third time."

A peek at Sam confirmed he'd heard. Annie's cheeks flamed at his amused smile. This was absolutely the last time she was taking her grandmother anywhere.

The mayor beckoned her over. "Annie, you have to see what Sam brought. You, too, Granny."

"Hurry," her grandmother encouraged when Annie dawdled.

"Yeah, hurry," Lyndsey echoed.

Annie meandered over, her calm exterior hiding the bundle of nerves that had become her stomach. When she would have stood next to the mayor, Granny squeezed by, leaving Annie no choice but to occupy the vacant space beside Sam.

She became intensely aware of his proximity. The fresh outdoor scent that clung to him, more intoxicating than any cologne. The warmth radiating off his skin. The pull of attraction impossible to resist.

No longer unreadable, his expression reflected a longing that her rapidly beating heart answered.

"This is simply incredible." The mayor had her head buried inside the box and was gushing over its contents. "What do you suppose is on these?" She came up for air, a wheel-shaped object clutched in her hands.

Annie was no expert, but she guessed it to be a reel of film. The other committee members had started to gather around as well.

"It's from *The Forty-Niners*," Sam said. "Or, so we think."

"I found the box in the back of a closet shelf." Irma brushed her fingers along the side of the box, leaving lines in the thick dust.

"This is quite a discovery." The mayor handled the reel of film as if it were a priceless artifact.

"There are some photographs, too." Sam reached into the

box for one. "You may want this." He passed the picture to Granny.

She gasped softly. "My word! Can't believe I was ever that young."

Annie studied the photo, mesmerized. The closest she'd seen her grandmother in love was when she reminisced about those days. Here it was in black-and-white.

What Annie would give to experience a love like that. Experience it again. With Sam.

Only he was leaving. In a matter of days, according to her mother.

He might delay his departure if she asked him.

Finding out would put Annie at risk. If she was mistaken, she'd be in for another loss. One she might not recover from. Annie stepped back.

"Can I have this?" Granny Orla asked Sam.

"You should go through the box. Take as many as you want."

"What about the film reels?" The mayor had yet to relinquish the one she held.

"I'm hoping to have them restored and transferred to a more durable media. And if there's no copyright issue, I'll show the film to tourists at the ranch. Same with the photographs. Add a few to the ones already hanging in the parlor. The rest…" He paused and didn't continue until Annie looked at him. "The rest are for the memorial."

The distance she'd placed between them magically narrowed. When he next spoke, they were inches apart.

"What you're doing," he said, "donating your land and the insurance money for the memorial, it's pretty wonderful. And very brave."

"I'm glad to do it."

"Won't you miss the inn?"

"Working for the NDF isn't so bad. At least I don't have to deal with cranky guests all day long."

"You're making a huge sacrifice. Your family, too."

"Fiona likes working at the ranch," Granny Orla interjected. "So don't you be laying her off anytime soon."

"No fear of that. Who else would run the place for me? Unless you're willing to come out of retirement."

She dismissed him with a wave. "Not much of that. Though I might be talked into volunteering at the memorial now and then. Being old does have its advantages. Aren't many folks who know more of the town's history than me."

"What about giving tours at the ranch house?" Sam asked. "When we reopen it to the public. Like Mrs. Litey used to."

"I'm not up to a full-time job. These joints of mine give me too much grief."

"However many hours you want. I'm flexible."

"I'd like that." Joy spread across her face. "I've had my fill of cranky guests, too."

"I can't vouch for the tourists who will visit the ranch," Sam said.

"If they're fans of the show, we'll get along fine."

"I want to help give tours," Lyndsey piped up.

"You can be my assistant." Granny put an affectionate arm around the girl. "When you visit."

"Daddy, can't we stay longer? Please."

"Maybe. I need to talk to Annie first." If only they weren't surrounded by people.

"You've done so much for me and my family," she said. "I'm running out of ways to say thank-you."

His mouth curved up at the corners in a sexy grin. "I can think of one or two."

So could she. "We could talk, I suppose."

"That, too." He lowered his head.

"Wait!" She placed her hands flat on his chest.

"Why? No one's watching."

She looked over in time to see Granny Orla ushering everyone up the basement stairs. She and Sam were alone.

When he pulled her into his arms and kissed her hungrily, she gladly and freely let go of her remaining doubts and insecurities. Whatever challenges lay ahead, they would conquer them together.

"I thought I'd lost you," he said, dragging his mouth away from hers.

"Me, too."

Another kiss, this one stealing her breath. "I swear to you, Annie Hennessy, I won't disappoint you." He kept her tucked inside the circle of his arms. "I'm here for the long haul."

"If not, I'd have to chase after you to California."

"You'd do that?"

"I'm here for the long haul, too." She pressed closer to him.

"Your mom and Granny Orla are happy in the apartment. Why don't you keep it for them?"

"But we found a bigger place."

He rested his chin on the top of her head. "I want you and Nessa to live with me at the Gold Nugget."

"Sam…"

"Think about it, at least. There's plenty of room. More when the cabin's built. You've always wanted the ranch. Now you can have it. And me."

She cupped his cheek with her hand. "I wouldn't move there just for the ranch."

"God, I hope not."

"It's a big decision."

"Let me sweeten the pot." He took her hand and turned it palm up, then kissed the sensitive center. "Marry me, Annie Hennessey."

"Sam!"

"Today. Tomorrow. As soon as possible. The mayor can perform the ceremony."

"We can't get married on the spot."

"Sure we can. This is Sweetheart, Nevada. A place where people have married on the spot for generations."

She laughed. A giddy, light-headed sort of laugh. "You're crazy, you know."

"I've wanted to marry you from the moment I saw you riding that bike on Cohea Ridge."

She didn't think her feelings for Sam could grow. But they did, filling every corner of her heart.

"Let's not waste any more time," he said. "I want to be a family. You, me, Lyndsey and Nessa. Maybe one more. I wouldn't mind a boy."

"Slow down! Let's not get too far ahead of ourselves."

"You don't want more children?"

She softened. "There's nothing I'd like more than to have a child with you. But we have a guest ranch to build."

"The best working guest ranch in the entire western United States," Sam boasted.

Well, he deserved to boast.

"We'll pass it on to our children," she said. "Along with the memorial."

"Deal. There won't be just one heart of Sweetheart, there'll be two. Yours and mine."

"You drive a hard bargain."

"Say yes, Annie. I'll make you happy, I swear."

"I do like the menagerie you've collected. Especially the goats."

"I hate the goats."

"I know."

Taking his hand, she led him up the stairs and outside. The same crowd from below greeted them.

"Well?" Granny Orla demanded, hands on her hips. "Are you ready to make an honest woman out of my granddaughter?"

"Yeah." Lyndsey mimicked the older woman.

"Past ready," Sam assured them. "But she's dragging her feet."

"What's wrong with you, girl? Have you lost your marbles?"

Annie made them wait a few seconds longer before wrapping her arms around Sam's waist. "Yes, I'll marry you. Of course I will."

She lost track of the hugs and congratulations after that. Except for Lyndsey's. Hers was the most poignant.

"I always wanted a little sister," she said.

Annie melted on the spot.

Mayor Dempsey offered to host the reception, free of charge. More offers followed, for catering, flowers and decorations.

"When's the happy occasion?" the mayor asked.

"Soon, I hope."

Sam wasn't the only anxious one. The others were equally eager for the first wedding since the fire.

"Fine, fine." With an exaggerated groan, Annie caved to the pressure. "Three weeks from Saturday."

"Three weeks?" Sam's grin collapsed.

"After the cattle roundup. You have to go back for that."

"We'll get married first. Then I'll leave."

"Sam!"

"For crying out loud," Granny Orla grumbled. "Put the poor man out of his misery."

"Two weeks from Saturday then."

"This Saturday," Sam insisted. "And you and Nessa fly back with Lyndsey and me for the roundup."

Before Annie quite knew what was happening, her wedding date was decided.

Sam pulled Irma aside. "Can you give Granny a ride home and watch Lyndsey for a while?"

"Take your time. No hurrying on my account."

Granny kissed Sam soundly on the cheek before leaving with Irma. "Welcome to the family, son."

Sam immediately steered Annie to his truck.

"Where are we going?"

"To celebrate. At the ranch."

Instead of taking her inside the house, they headed to the barn and up to the loft.

There, atop a pile of fresh, sweet-smelling hay, they reminisced about the past, planned for the future and made incredible love.

Well after dark, Sam returned Annie home so they could break the news to her mother and Nessa. At the door to the apartment, he stopped her in order to pluck a few stray stalks of hay from her hair and apparently missed a few.

Fiona noticed and commented. Annie was too happy to care.

Epilogue

Annie stood at the top of the stairs, one hand resting on the banister, the other clutching a bouquet of fresh-picked wildflowers. At the bottom of the stairs, her grandmother waited, smiling brilliantly. She was there to walk Annie down the aisle.

The aisle, such as it was, consisted of the short distance across the parlor, between two dozen white folding chairs. Her and Sam's closest friends and family occupied the chairs. Later, during the reception at the Paydirt Saloon, half the town was expected to show up.

It seemed fitting, marrying Sam—the love of her life— here, at the Gold Nugget. A place important to them both. A place they'd always loved. Where their future and those of their children stretched ahead of them.

Hard to imagine, seven weeks ago, that she and Sam had met again on these very stairs, only then he had stood at the top and she at the bottom. So much had happened in that incredibly short time. And, yet, they were where they should be: at the end of a journey that had started eleven years earlier.

Annie descended the stairs. Stepping daintily from the last step, she linked arms with her grandmother.

"Nervous?"

"No. This is one of the best days of my life."

"That's my girl." Granny Orla patted Annie's hand. "You look stunning."

"Thank you."

The dress had been loaned to her by the school principal's wife. Mayor Dempsey was officiating the ceremony. The decorations were courtesy of the Sweetheart Memorial committee members. Lyndsey's and Nessa's frilly flower girl dresses had been sewn in record time by Linda Lee. *Linda Lee,* not Gary's new wife.

Having finally found her own happy ending, Annie wished nothing but the best for her ex. He deserved more than she'd ever been able to give him.

Everyone stood as she entered the parlor, their faces beaming. Annie had invited the head of the wildlife refuge where Daffy Duck and Porky Pig resided, the pair now fat, healthy raccoon cubs. Lyndsey would be volunteering there once or twice a month with Gus. She'd recently proclaimed she wanted to be a veterinarian when she grew up. Living Annie's dream.

Annie had no problem with that. She was too content living her own dream.

Speaking of which...

The girls, adorable in their dresses with matching wildflower bouquets, stood beside Annie's mother, who served as her maid of honor. Sam's parents had flown in for the wedding, along with his brother, the best man. Also at the wedding was Lyndsey's grandfather.

Annie thought it must be difficult for him to watch his former son-in-law marry another woman. It was quite a testament to their friendship and the man's character.

She'd liked him instantly and, after noticing the interested and frequent glances between him and her mother, invited him back for a visit in the very near future.

Her gaze wandered to the makeshift altar near the large picture window. At the sight of Sam in his dress Western suit and polished black boots, her mind emptied of all save him. He was that same young man she'd first glimpsed on horseback, only incredibly more handsome.

Handing off her bouquet to her grandmother, she clasped hands with him.

To her shock and surprise, he hauled her against him and kissed her senseless.

The room let out a collective gasp, then erupted in whoops and hollers.

"Hey," the mayor protested with feigned irritation when the noise died down. "You have to wait till the I-pronounce-you-man-and-wife part before kissing your bride."

Sam looked longingly and lovingly into Annie's eyes. "I couldn't."

The mayor answered with a sparkle in her voice. "Considering how long it's taken the two of you to get here, I guess we can let you slide."

Sam kissed Annie again when the ceremony was over. Sweeping her up into his arms, he carried her over the threshold—not inside but outside. Onto the porch. There, he set her on her feet and enveloped her in the most exquisite of embraces.

"I love you, Mrs. Wyler."

Mrs. Wyler. That had a nice ring to it. "I love you, too."

"We're going to have an amazing life together."

She rose on tiptoes and pressed her lips to his, pouring all the love she'd felt for him into that single moment.

Annie would always miss her family's inn. But together she and Sam would build something even greater and of more importance. For the town, for their family and most especially for themselves.

* * * * *

*Watch for the next story in the Sweetheart,
Nevada trilogy, HIS CHRISTMAS SWEETHEART,
coming November 2013,
only from Harlequin American Romance.*

REQUEST YOUR FREE BOOKS!
2 FREE NOVELS PLUS 2 FREE GIFTS!

HARLEQUIN

American ★ Romance®

LOVE, HOME & HAPPINESS

YES! Please send me 2 FREE Harlequin® American Romance® novels and my 2 FREE gifts (gifts are worth about $10). After receiving them, if I don't wish to receive any more books, I can return the shipping statement marked "cancel." If I don't cancel, I will receive 4 brand-new novels every month and be billed just $4.74 per book in the U.S. or $5.24 per book in Canada. That's a savings of at least 14% off the cover price! It's quite a bargain! Shipping and handling is just 50¢ per book in the U.S. and 75¢ per book in Canada.* I understand that accepting the 2 free books and gifts places me under no obligation to buy anything. I can always return a shipment and cancel at any time. Even if I never buy another book, the two free books and gifts are mine to keep forever.

154/354 HDN F4YN

Name _____ (PLEASE PRINT) _____

Address _____ Apt. # _____

City _____ State/Prov. _____ Zip/Postal Code _____

Signature (if under 18, a parent or guardian must sign) _____

Mail to the **Harlequin® Reader Service:**
IN U.S.A.: P.O. Box 1867, Buffalo, NY 14240-1867
IN CANADA: P.O. Box 609, Fort Erie, Ontario L2A 5X3

Want to try two free books from another line?
Call 1-800-873-8635 or visit www.ReaderService.com.

* Terms and prices subject to change without notice. Prices do not include applicable taxes. Sales tax applicable in N.Y. Canadian residents will be charged applicable taxes. Offer not valid in Quebec. This offer is limited to one order per household. Not valid for current subscribers to Harlequin American Romance books. All orders subject to credit approval. Credit or debit balances in a customer's account(s) may be offset by any other outstanding balance owed by or to the customer. Please allow 4 to 6 weeks for delivery. Offer available while quantities last.

Your Privacy—The Harlequin® Reader Service is committed to protecting your privacy. Our Privacy Policy is available online at www.ReaderService.com or upon request from the Harlequin Reader Service.

We make a portion of our mailing list available to reputable third parties that offer products we believe may interest you. If you prefer that we not exchange your name with third parties, or if you wish to clarify or modify your communication preferences, please visit us at www.ReaderService.com/consumerschoice or write to us at Harlequin Reader Service Preference Service, P.O. Box 9062, Buffalo, NY 14269. Include your complete name and address.

HAR13R

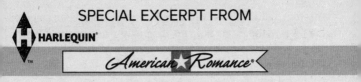

SPECIAL EXCERPT FROM

HARLEQUIN®

American ★ Romance®

THE LONG, HOT TEXAS SUMMER
by *Cathy Gillen Thacker*

The second book in the McCABE HOMECOMING *series.*

Welcome back to Laramie County, Texas, where things are heating up between Justin McCabe and his new carpenter!

There were times for doing-it-yourself and times for not, Justin McCabe thought grimly, surveying the damage he had just inadvertently inflicted on a brand-new utility cabinet.

It was possible, of course, this could be fixed, without buying a whole new cabinet. If he knew what he was doing. Which he did not—a fact the five beloved ranch mutts, sitting quietly, cautiously watching his every move, seemed to realize, too.

A motor sounded in the lane.

Hoping it was the carpenter who was supposed to be there that morning, Justin walked to the door of Bunkhouse #1, just as a fancy red extended-cab Silverado pickup truck pulled up in front of the lodge. It had an equally elaborate travel trailer attached to the back. A lone woman was at the wheel.

"Great." Justin sighed as all the dogs darted out of the open door of the partially finished bunkhouse and raced, barking their heads off, toward her.

The lost tourist eased the window down and stuck her head out into the sweltering Texas heat. A straw hat with a sassily rolled brim perched on her head. Sunglasses shaded her eyes. But there was no disguising her beautiful face. With her sexy shoulders and incredibly buff bare arms, the interloper was, without a doubt, the most staggeringly beautiful female Justin had ever seen.

She smiled at the dogs. "Hey, poochies," she greeted them softly and melodically.

As entranced as he was, they simply sat down and stared.

She opened her door and stepped out. All six feet of her.

A double layer of red-and-white tank tops showcased her nice, full breasts and slender waist. A short denim skirt clung to her hips and showcased a pair of really fine legs. Her equally sexy feet were encased in a pair of red flip flops.

She took off her hat and shook out a mane of butterscotch hair that fell in soft waves past her shoulders. She turned and tossed the hat on the seat behind her, then reached down to pet his five rescue dogs in turn. The pack was thoroughly besotted.

Justin completely understood.

If there was such a thing as love at first sight—which he knew there wasn't—he'd be a goner.

THE LONG, HOT TEXAS SUMMER
by Cathy Gillen Thacker.
Available August 6, 2013,
from Harlequin® American Romance®.
And watch for two more books in the series this summer!

HAREXP0813